CREEPERS

JESSE HAYNES

CREEPERS

TATE PUBLISHING
AND ENTERPRISES, LLC

Published by Tate Publishing & Enterprises, LLC
127 E. Trade Center Terrace | Mustang, Oklahoma 73064 USA
1.888.361.9473 | www.tatepublishing.com

Tate Publishing is committed to excellence in the publishing industry. The company reflects the philosophy established by the founders, based on Psalm 68:11,
"The Lord gave the word and great was the company of those who published it."

Book design copyright © 2014 by Tate Publishing, LLC. All rights reserved.
Cover design by Junriel Boquecosa
Interior design by Manolito Bastasa

Published in the United States of America

ISBN: 978-1-63185-358-6
Fiction / Science Fiction / Alien Contact
14.09.02

To Deborah Branscum,
Who inspired my love for writing in the fourth grade.

CHAPTER 1

I t was in a small room on the top floor of the New York City hospital that the men had chosen to assemble. They all had arrived just before nine o'clock in the morning, carrying briefcases and dressed in their finest suits. Each of the seven men had been invited by the resident doctor, Winston Falons, who was the most revered and respected medical practitioner in the state of New York. The other men were of similar reputation, but they specialized in many different fields. The eight men sitting in the small room were considered to be the most brilliant medical minds in the United States, and they had all been contacted for this meeting to discuss a special yet grave occurrence.

A hospital secretary walked into the room carrying a box of pastries. She sat the box in the middle of the expensive mahogany table the men had gathered around. None of the doctors moved. They gazed upon the box of pastries with solemn expressions that hid their whirling and stirring medical minds, which were more confused than ever before. The room was uncomfortably silent.

Dr. Falons, dressed in his finest suit and wearing his signature golden Rolex wristwatch, sat at the head of the table, studying medical files intently while the other men arrived. At last, he spoke, "Gentlemen, I appreciate every single one of you coming to meet with me today." He sounded tired as he spoke, but he continued, "I don't believe that this much medical expertise has ever been assembled in the same room at one time. If we are going to find the answer to this sinister medical emergency, then it will come today."

The seven other men nodded. Dr. White, a lung specialist, asked, "Will you give us complete background information on your patient, Dr. Falons?"

Falons took a manila folder from in front of him and opened it. He extracted page after page of notes taken in his own shaky handwriting and began to read aloud, "My patient, C. J. Sanders, checked into the hospital in a vegetative state twenty days ago. Exactly one month ago today, he was in space, aboard a United States space station, where he apparently contracted this mysterious sickness." Falons paused as the other doctors began to scribble notes onto their personal pads of paper. He waited for any questions, but none came. He continued, "Sanders was in space when he became sick. His symptoms were delirium, moments of intense rage, confusion, and dizziness. The symptoms only lasted for twenty-four hours before he went into a coma. The doctors on the station couldn't figure out what was wrong, and he was then sent here because the case became a priority."

The heart specialist, Dr. Miles, said, "That is incredibly fast. For all of the symptoms to set in as quickly as they did and force the host into a coma, there must have been some sort of catalyst. Was the fact that he was in space a factor in making the sickness attack so quickly?"

Falons answered with a simple, "I'm not sure." Realizing further explanation was wanted, he continued, "I have tested Sanders for anything that could possibly trigger the symptoms. Still, I have found nothing." He took a slide from within the manila folder and stood. The doctor walked to a large window that overlooked New York City, pressing the slide against the window so that it was illuminated with natural light. The image in the slide glowed, and Falons said, "This slide is the latest MRI of my patient's head. Please note the brain."

The brain specialist of the group, Darren Edlemon, exclaimed, "What brain? There is nothing left, or at least nothing that seems active!"

"Yes," replied Falons, "the sickness has, for a lack of a better term, shut down over three-quarters of the patient's brain. I am at a loss as to how he is still alive."

Edlemon now seemed to have taken an even more special interest to this case. He declared, "Well, for the patient's brain to be destroyed at such a quick rate, there is only one thing I can think of that would do such a thing."

All eight of the doctors in the room spoke in unison, "A virus."

"Exactly," continued Falons. "The only answer to the problem is that our patient has contracted some kind of extraterrestrial virus. That is as much as I know. There is little we can do for him. He will remain a vegetable until his death. Our job is to figure out this extraterrestrial virus—what feeds it, what it responds to, how it reproduces and spreads, and, particularly, how to combat it. My patient is being quarantined, but if we are not careful, then this could turn into a global epidemic."

An Indian man, Dr. Rasheem, asked, "All right, so where do we begin?"

"I figure the best place to start would be evaluating the patient firsthand. I feel that you need to see him in person. So which of you men would like to join me for the first trip? We have five biohazard suits to use, so I'll need four others. Any volunteers?"

Four hands shot into the air like school children. They were the hands of Edlemon, Miles, Rasheem, and Dr. Samuel Cooney, who was the expert virologist. The other three men looked uncertain as to what they should do.

Falons helped them. "All right, the four of you who volunteered should follow me to the patient's room while the other three can review the patient's medical history. I left a folder containing the patient's background and the analysis of the recent tests on the table right there." He pointed to a thick file folder on the table. "Gentlemen, let's go."

Falons and the rest of the doctors who were joining him stood. As the three doctors who were staying behind began to examine the patient's medical history, Falons's group left the meeting room. They walked from the meeting room and out into a long corridor bustling with nurses, doctors, and people pushing gurneys. The five brilliant men set off purposefully down the hallway. None of them spoke as they followed Falons around bends and through doors. Eventually, the doctors ended up outside a hospital room with tall windows and no apparent exit. The blinds were shut, so it was impossible to see into the room.

"Follow me," said Falons. He went inside two double doors, and the four other doctors followed. They stepped into the decontamination room, from where they took biohazard suits and put them on. The suits resembled a space suit—large white full-body suits that came complete with a round helmet and air mask.

Once everyone was wearing the protective suit, Falons continued, "We shall now evaluate the patient. I want all of you to be comfortable and treat him as if he was your own patient. Everyone's opinion matters. That is why you are all here."

"Very well then," said Cooney, his voice slightly distorted by the suit. "I think I can speak for everyone here in that we are very willing to help. This is an exceptionally rare case, and none of us would want to miss out. I doubt anyone has experimented with an extraterrestrial virus such as this."

Edlemon agreed, "Yes, I was very intrigued by this case as well. Please, Dr. Falons, lead the way."

"All right," said Falons, "but do not be surprised by the current state of the patient. The virus has had many, um, interesting effects." With that, he opened the door to the patient's room and walked inside.

The sight before the four unprepared doctors came as a complete shock. Two doctors gasped at what they saw. The patient was lying on the hospital bed with his eyes closed, arms tucked by his sides, and legs covered by a blanket, yet he barely looked human. The body of the former astronaut had changed in many ways. His skin had gone to a horribly ugly pale color, more like a sheet of paper than a living person. The patient's hair was patchy and mangled; most of it had fallen out. Even more peculiar, he had lost almost all of his body fat, yet his muscles seemed to protrude and show thick veins underneath the pale skin. A heart rate monitor connected to him showed hardly anything more than a straight line.

Falons led the procession of doctors across the room and beside the bed. He said, "It only gets more interesting from here." Reaching toward the patient's head, Falons said, "Keep in mind that Sanders had light blue eyes." He pulled back the eyelids, and the other four doctors gasped at the same time. The patient's eyes had changed completely. The pupils had contracted, and the iris had changed into a frightening mix of orange and yellow. "I'm not sure what caused that."

"That is unbelievable," gasped Rasheem.

"Well, look at this." Now Falons pulled back Sander's pale lips to reveal the teeth, which had somehow transformed as well. Instead of being cubed and smooth like an average human's, the patient's teeth had become sharp and jagged. Rows of sharp fangs jutted from his gums. "The virus caused extra calcium to be produced, and most of it went to the host's teeth. His bones have also become denser. Experiments indicate that they are about three times stronger than average."

"I don't believe it," said Miles.

"Look at his muscles," continued Cooney.

"Yes," Falons replied, pointing at his patient's arm. He prodded a swollen bicep, which twitched in response to the stimulation. "Once again, the virus has also changed the amount of proteins the body produces. It seems to use the patient's fat and break it down, using the calories to produce proteins that go straight to the muscles."

Rasheem asked, "What effect would that have on the patient? If he were conscious and functional, I mean."

Still prodding different muscles, Falons explained, "The best explanation I can think of is this: Imagine intense weight training and using muscle gain supplements for around three years. The patient has gone through the same transformation in about three weeks. If he were coherent and functional, then his strength would be miraculous."

Edlemon, who was leaning over the patient's head and examining the yellow eyes for himself, added, "So this man has become, well…"

"He's like the ultimate predator," Falons finished the sentence. "He's as strong as a bodybuilder, and he has a mouthful of fangs. Yet he's in a vegetative state with half of a brain." Until he had put it like that, the doctor hadn't realized just how creepy the situation was.

Everyone else in the room seemed to feel the same way. There was silence, and all five men stepped away from the comatose body. A sinister presence seemed to hang in the room over the motionless man lying out-stretched on the hospital bed.

Cooney broke the silence. "Do you know what that sounds like?"

More awkward silence came.

Finally, Miles spoke the word on everyone's mind, "A zombie."

With that, laughter broke loose. In the room were five of the most brilliant medical minds in the world, and with that came unparalleled rationality. The idea of a zombie virus, which all of the men had heard about and seen in movies, was completely absurd. All the doctors felt a twinge of subconscious discontent in that they had allowed the thought of a zombie to enter their minds. Despite the briefness the idea lasted, the count-less years the doctors had spent in medical school made even hosting the absurd idea an embarrassment.

Falons knew it was time to change the subject. "How do you think we should proceed? I have honestly given up all hope of the patient living, and so has his family. They haven't even seen him since he's looked like this. Anyway, I have been keeping him alive for the sake of experimentation. We must learn how to fight this virus so that it won't spread."

"Yes, you are right." Cooney asked, "Can I take a blood sample?" Falons nodded his permission and then the blood expert set to work.

Rasheem was studying the heart rate monitor intently. He stated, "The patient barely has a pulse."

"His heart has been beating about thirty-five times a minute, which is about half of the average amount of beats for a slumbering person."

"That is ridiculous," marveled Cooney as he stuck the patience with a syringe to draw blood.

Rasheem burst out, "Whoa, look at this!" All the men looked toward the heart rate monitor, which had suddenly began displaying more movement.

"His pulse is improving. He's…he's responding to the needle."

"I don't believe it!"

"Maybe he's coming out of the coma."

In a rush, the entire group of doctors gathered around the vegetative body. Cooney took the needle from the man's arm, but the heart rate didn't drop. It was actually climbing on the screen before the doctor's eyes. All of the doctors were so engrossed in the heart monitor that none of them saw two yellow eyes snap open.

The three doctors who had stayed behind in the room to review the patient's medical history were very busy at work. The work was cut short, however, by the screams and shrieks echoing from the corridor. The men stood at once.

A woman's voice came, "Help us, dear God! The patient has escaped!"

Dr. White ran to the door, with the other two doctors, Keene and Lincoln, following him closely behind.

"That must have been one hell of a patient." He glanced quizzically at his accompanying doctors, but none of them seemed to know anything.

They stepped into the hallway and froze in place, facing something that seemed to come straight from a horror movie. Thirty feet down the hallway was some kind of monster. It was stooped over with inhumanly pale skin, humanoid in form but with the posture of a Neanderthal from the evolution of man chart. The thing had shabby hair and piercing yellow eyes. It had a long object in its mouth, but White couldn't identify what the object was.

Lincoln asked, "What is that thing?"

Keene said, "That's Falons's watch!"

White didn't know what Keene was talking about. He knew exactly what Falons's watch looked like, for it was a beautiful golden Rolex, but he didn't see it anywhere. His mind was buzzing with questions and even a feeling of fear. Suddenly, he spotted the watch, and he immediately wished that he hadn't. The object in the monster's mouth was an arm, a detached human arm complete with a string of tendons and ligaments where the shoulder should be. On the wrist of the arm glittered a golden Rolex.

Shuddering, White comprehended just what was going on. This *thing* must have formerly been the astronaut that had been affected with the virus. He had somehow mutated into this savage beast. The entire situation seemed like something from a science fiction movie, but the beast seemed very real.

In a flash, the mutant dashed forward at the three doctors. The grown men all screamed like little children and turned to run away. The men, dressed in suits and leather shoes, were no match for the monster, which seemed to have superhuman speed. It spit Falons's arm to the ground and then leapt at Dr. Keene. He was knocked from his feet to the linoleum tiles with the beast on top of him. Opening its mouth to expose sharp fangs, the beast sank its teeth into the doctor's shoulder.

Lincoln yelled, "Run! Don't look back."

A police officer rounded a corner in front of the scrambling doctors. He had his gun raised and trained on the monster, which was spitting and hissing profusely. The officer yelled, "Freeze," but it had no effect on the mutant. Lincoln and White ran past him, but the monster didn't. Instead, it attacked him, biting his leg and slinging the relatively large man into the wall seemingly effortlessly. The crumpled body of the officer landed in a heap, and the pistol skidded away.

White kept running, vaguely aware that the monster was getting dangerously close. From the corner of his eye, he saw Lincoln attacked from behind and downed in mere seconds. White turned to see sharp fangs sinking into Lincoln's neck. That was when he knew that it was all over.

The next series of events was a blur. In seconds, the monster was on top of White, who wasn't even certain as to how he had ended up on the ground. He felt the fangs sink into his chest as he stared into the yellow eyes that loomed above him. He heard gunfire and saw two holes tear through the monster's chest. It pitched and wailed before collapsing on top of White, who was clutching his wound.

Screams came. "Someone, anyone! Get medical attention immediately! We need help."

White groaned. The bite wound in his chest was painful and bleeding terribly. Still, he knew it was only a flesh wound and wouldn't kill him, especially since he was in a hospital. There was another thought though, dark and sinister, which seemed to persist in the back of his mind. He tried to push it away, but the thought refused to go. Finally, White admitted his worst fear— if this patient had mutated into the monster because of a virus, then the virus may have been transferred to him through the bite. The same mutant fate possibly awaited White, and he knew that the only choice was to wait and find out. He clutched his wound and muttered, "It's just a virus. How bad could it get?"

CHAPTER 2

FIVE YEARS LATER

It happened once a month. A plane would fly above New York City and drop a crate, which a parachute would aid in a slow descent and a soft landing. It would typically land in Central Park, but that was never certain. Today, for instance, the crate had landed in the middle of Broadway Street.

Jason and Drake Bennett slowly advanced down the street to where they'd seen the crate land. The formerly magnificent towers of New York City loomed over them and blocked out the fading evening sun. Shadows were cast down on the abandoned cars that littered New York City. Weeds and stalks of grass poked through the cracks in Broadway Street, which had become decrepit with nobody left to tend to it.

The brothers didn't know of another single survivor apart from each other that was uninfected by the Space Virus, as the sickness had been coined by the medical professionals who had died studying it. They didn't have much time for researching it either, as the virus had spread to 80 percent of the United States in less than six months. The gruesome virus did unimaginable things to the host, things even worse than death. The host would eventually die, but only after months of gruesome changes. Now there was only a tiny percentage of earth's population left, or at least that was Jason's estimation. That percentage, however, was almost entirely composed of mutants.

Jason held his hand to his side in a way that implied he wanted his younger brother to stop. His sharp features tensed, and he strained his eyes against the bright sun as he looked across the street. He whispered, "I think I heard something. Be prepared." Both Jason and Drake raised their machine guns, which were shiny AK-47s. The assault rifles were capable of firing ten rounds per second, but even that sometimes wouldn't seem like enough in the middle of an attack.

The brothers kneeled down behind a taxi that had been abandoned in the middle of the street sometime ago. Drake, who was sixteen, always listened to his eighteen-year-old brother in situations like these. They occasionally fought with each other like typical brothers, but as far as they knew, they were the only two remaining humans left in the entire state of New York, so they usually appreciated each other's company. At times, it was this company that was the only reason they'd survived to this point.

After hunkering down for over two minutes, Drake murmured, "I think it's clear. We can move." His brother nodded and stood, but with his rifle still cautiously raised. Checking his ammunition clip, Drake said, "I need to get some ammunition magazines today, I'm running low on bullets."

Jason sarcastically replied, "Well, now's a beautiful time to mention this. What if we were to get attacked right now?"

Pulling his worn leather jacket back to reveal the 9 mm handgun that was clipped to his belt, Drake answered, "I'll be fine. I can still shoot, just not as fast."

They gingerly advanced forward. By now, the supply crate was visible in the distance. It had landed perfectly in the bed of a white truck before the parachute had settled over the vehicle. These crates were the only sign that there were other humans uninfected by the Space Virus. Somewhere, there had to be people building these crates and packing them with food, medical supplies, and weapons before they were dropped off by plane. Jason had tried to catch the pilot's attention several times by climbing onto the roof of the hotel building that they were living in, but so far, he hadn't succeeded.

From a far distance, to the east, came an inhuman scream. The cry was high-pitched and drawn out. It was a sound that always managed to make the hairs on the back of the boys' necks stand on end in fear. Drake said the one word that was on both of the brothers' minds—"creepers."

Creepers was the name that had been given to the people infected with the Space Virus. Jason could remember his friends joking about a zombie apocalypse years ago, as if it was something out of a comic book. Now, it had somehow come true, or at least almost come true. Creepers were different from zombies in many ways. Jason and his brother were far from experts on the mutants and the virus that caused them, but they had picked up on a few things. Zombies were supposed to be mindless and slow-moving, and they were supposed to target the brains of victims. They supposedly only moved at night, as far as Jason remembered from back when he had a television.

Creepers were much worse. They were quick and lean savages with the sole mental focus of spreading the disease at whatever cost, at any time of day. The only way the disease could be spread was through saliva and bites, therefore, creepers would always bite their victim so the virus could take over the new host.

Upon the bite, the new host would transform into something that was certainly not human. The transformation would start out slowly. First, the virus would attack the host's brain, killing the majority of the cells and leaving only enough for the host to be capable of basic body functions. Then the host would change in appearance; his or her skin would become pale and seemingly contract. All of the body fat would rot away, and the muscles would gain a bulging appearance. Adding to the hideous appearance was the eyes, which would change to a bright yellow. It was these gleaming yellow eyes that would haunt many of Jason and Drake's dreams.

There was another scream of a creeper in the distance, this one perhaps coming in response to the first. Creepers usually attacked in packs, but the only way they seemed to communicate was through screaming, roaring, and hissing sounds.

Drake was listening intently to the wails when Jason spoke, "Let's hope they stay where they are. C'mon, let's run." He took off in a dead sprint through the streets. Drake followed closely behind, struggling to keep up with his older brother. Both brothers were almost impossibly fit, for that was what it took to survive. Still, Jason was taller, and he could run faster than Drake with his long stride.

They ran for half a minute before they reached the supply crate in the back of the truck. Jason hoped that the sounds of their shoes slapping against the ground wouldn't attract the creepers, but there was always that possibility. The boys climbed into the bed of the truck, and Drake took a long military-grade knife from the vest he was wearing. He used it to slice through the parachute attached to the supply crate. He pulled the parachute from the crate while Jason stood on the tailgate and watched for movement coming from any dark alley between two skyscrapers. Creepers would come from anywhere, and they never failed to surprise.

Fighting to pry the lid off of the crate with nothing but his gloved hands, Drake said, "Hey, help me out." Jason turned and pushed his sweaty dark hair away from his eyes before helping his younger brother remove the lid from the crate. It pried away easily with the combined strength of both teenage boys. As usual, the crate was filled with survival necessities. Food was on top; most of it was canned meats and vegetables. Both Jason and Drake wore satchels, which they began stuffing with the cans. There was even a loaf of fresh bread in the crate that Jason carefully placed in his satchel. The food in the crate was what the boys always relied on because the creepers had broke into and raided all of the homes and grocery stores. However, the Bennett brothers never took all of the food from the crate, just in case there were other survivors in the enormous city, even though they knew that this hope was probably misplaced.

After rummaging through the food and taking all that they could hold, the boys moved to the medical supplies packed underneath. Their personal supply was large, so they didn't need to take much, but Jason still took a bottle of hydrogen peroxide and some gauze. Both he and his brother had been scratched by creepers several times, but fortunately, neither of them had been bitten. The peroxide was always useful for disinfecting the scratches, so the brother's supply of it could never grow too large.

Finally, buried under Band-Aids and ibuprofen pills were the weapons. There were knives of various sizes and several miscellaneous firearms. The mysterious benefactor who'd been leaving the boys these supply crates seemed to have great taste in weaponry. Jason spotted what he believed to be an FAL, and he pulled it from the crate and then strapped it to his back. Drake took several magazines of bullets that could be loaded into his AK-47.

"I think that is all that I need," said Drake while he rummaged through the remaining contents of the

24

crate. His brother was sliding the lid back into place when something caught Drake's eye. "Wait!"

Jason questioned, "What is it? We need to go. You know as well as I do that the creepers will be showing up soon. And keep your voice down."

Drake reached back into the crate and took out a manila envelope. He held it in his hands as if he was weighing the contents. "I've never seen one of these in there." He opened it and took out a single piece of paper.

Jason snatched the sheet away. "What is this? What does it say?" The side of the paper was blank, so he flipped it over. On the back of the paper, written in ink, were two words. "Miami, Florida," both brothers read the words aloud at the same time.

Suddenly, a rare feeling welled up inside Drake. It was a feeling of excitement. With a newfound hope, he asked, "Do you know what this is? There are people in Miami! They sent us this as a sign. How far is that from here?" Shoving the paper in his pocket, he looked up at his brother, whose eyes seemed to be gazing right though him. Jason had no doubt spotted something that he didn't like, and Drake knew that this could only mean one thing.

Turning, Drake saw what his brother had been intently staring at. A pack of creepers, nine in all, had emerged from inside one of the nearby buildings. They'd stay inside the majority of the time, but they certainly weren't afraid to come out and hunt in the middle of the day. All creepers were terrifying and ugly, but this group seemed even worse than usual. They were all larger than average, with pale sickly skin and sunken faces that gave them a rather skeletal appearance. Their lips curled back to reveal inhumanly long and sharp teeth. Creepers always walked in a way that they were hunched forward, with a curved back from which their spine seemed to protrude. They'd constantly smell the air, trying to sniff out prey. Apparently, the virus had heightened their sense of smell, along with sharpening their eyesight and hearing, turning them into ideal predators.

Jason slowly put his hand on Drake's shoulder. He whispered, "They haven't seen us yet. Let's lay down in the bed of the truck and maybe they'll leave."

In a desperate attempt to be as silent as possible, both brothers lowered their guns and went down on their knees. From there, they leaned forward onto their stomachs, sinking low enough in the bed of the truck that the creepers would not be able to see them. They were motionless, going as far as to hold their breath to reduce the noise that they made.

Jason estimated that the creepers were twenty-five yards away now. It was a windless day, and they were faintly audible as they hissed at each other. The sounds of their long fingernails scraping across the pavement or car doors could be heard, and each time, the noise seemed to be louder.

Drake urgently whispered, "They're coming our way! We need to do something." He fidgeted impatiently, clutching the AK-47 assault rifle against his battered maroon T-shirt.

Jason, more patient than his brother, said, "Maybe they still don't know we're here. Let's just wait it out.

Just because they are walking this way doesn't mean that they're after us."

"Well, what if they are? Do we only attack them when they're already on us?"

The question was interrupted as a snarl came from one of the creepers. It had to be only ten yards away now, still coming in the direction of the truck. The boys immediately stopped talking. By now, the sounds of the creepers' labored breathing could easily be made out. The scuttling sound of their cracked bare feet coming down the pavement was now a constant. The sounds were coming from directly beside the truck now. When things began to seem hopeless, the sounds instantly stopped.

Jason glanced at his brother, who now looked unimaginably tense. Maybe he'd been wrong, and the creepers were coming for them. A long and drawn out sniff came, piercing the terrifying silence. Certainly, the creeper had smelled the boys, and now they were both going to be attacked.

Then what happened next came as a surprise. The sounds of footfall resumed, and the creepers seemed to press forward. The scratching sound of one dragging its fingernail across the shut tailgate of the truck drew Jason's stomach into a knot. The hisses and breathing peaked in volume and then began growing slightly fainter as each footfall sounded. After over a minute, they were faint enough that Jason felt comfortable turning and sitting up in the bed of the truck.

Drake did the same, and they silently watched as the creepers continued to mindlessly wander across what used to be the iconic Broadway Street. The pack was loosely organized, and there seemed to be a lead creeper that the other eight were following. This creeper walked in the front of the pack, and it stood a head-and-shoulder taller than the others, as if it had been a professional basketball player before contracting the virus. It had bulging arms with broad shoulders, and the muscles in its legs rippled every time the beast took a step.

The pack of creepers was out of earshot before Drake muttered, "That has got to be the biggest one I've ever seen." He pointed the barrel of his rifle toward the lead creeper.

Jason nodded. "Yeah, he's huge. I'm so thankful that they didn't figure we were in the truck. I really thought that we were done for, and they certainly had the element of surprise on their side."

Despite the circumstances, a grin managed to stretch across Drake's face. With a sudden twinkle in his eyes, he stated, "Well, now we have the element of surprise in our favor."

"I guess you're right." Jason suddenly figured out what his brother was getting at. "Wait, you're not seriously considering attacking the creepers are you? Isn't it their job to attack us?"

Drake sighed. He looked around the abandoned street. The tall buildings that used to be so beautiful were now hideous. Half of the windows had been shattered. Moss and ivy were growing on the sides of many of them, and they were littered with graffiti images. "Do you remember when humanity started to fall? When everybody was getting the Space Virus and transforming into creepers?"

"I probably remember it better than you," Jason answered. "You were only eleven." He turned to look at the creepers, who had aimlessly begun digging in a garbage can.

Drake continued, "Do you remember when everyone thought that catching the virus was inescapable? Society didn't realize that it was only spread through bites, not aerially. I remember when people would run through the streets at night and yell for the creepers to take them. I even remember when half of the people at our apartment killed themselves to avoid becoming creepers."

"I remember that too, but I try to not think about those times." Jason closed his eyes as if he was visualizing the memories. "We've learned a lot on our own since then."

"That's my point. We know so much more about the creepers than they did. We know that they can die, and we also know how to kill them. You do realize that we can't continue living like this forever. At some point, we need to play offense. We need to attack them!" By now, Drake was talking a little louder than he should have.

Jason held his index finger to his lips. "Be quiet or they'll hear you."

"If they hear us and charge, we could cut them down with our guns before they even get too close. You know it's true." Drake's voice was even louder than it had been. "We've killed a hundred creepers."

Not wanting to alert them of their presence, Jason persisted, "Could you please be a little quieter? I know we've killed a lot of creepers, but we've been lucky. I'm trying to be cautious."

"Throw caution to the wind. I'm tired of living like this." Drake took the paper from his pocket and shoved it at Jason's face. "Read this! We're not alone anymore. There are people in Miami, so that's where we need to go!"

Sighing, Jason said, "I guess you're right, but I've felt alone in this world for so long that now I feel like I can't put hope in this Miami thing because I can't stand to have my hopes crushed again. What if we go to Miami and find nothing? Could we even get there?"

"Now's not the time to worry about it. Let's just kill these creepers, okay?" Drake looked to his brother and was rewarded with a hesitant nod. After a sigh from Jason, they both changed to a more combat-ready position. This meant assuming a crouched stance in the bed of the truck, with their body weight balanced on the balls of their feet.

Jason still was unsure about what his younger brother had persuaded him to do. He peered down the barrel of his AK-47 and trained it on the creeper to the far left. It was picking its teeth with long and dark fingernails. "I got the left. You start on the right."

"All right," Drake replied. "Three, two, one."

The explosion of gunfire rang out, made only louder by its echoing off of the tall skyscrapers. Jason's first bullet found its mark, striking the targeted creeper in the chest. The beast let out a pained wail as a fountain of blood blossomed into the air from the wound. It clutched the puncture in its bare chest, but the bleeding refused to let up. Jason took aim and sent three more bullets into the creeper, which collapsed in a heap.

Drake was also spraying bullets into the group of creepers that was about fifty yards away. Only six of the nine beasts were left by the time that the lead creeper realized where the bullets were coming from. It spotted the Bennett brothers and held out a hand in their direction, with an elongated finger pointed out. The other creepers followed with their gaze, and their eyes locked on to the gun-wielding humans. They all charged in unison. The creepers snarled as they sprinted directly at Jason and Drake.

"Take this," yelled Drake as he stood in the back of the truck and recklessly opened fire at the creepers. He stopped shooting after two more creepers fell and began bleeding out on the pavement.

Jason also began shooting at the creepers, but with a more focused effort than his brother. The first bullet he fired struck its target between the eyes. The muscular creeper howled as the bullet pierced its skull and tore through the remaining part of the brain that was still unaffected by the disease. Drake still wasn't shooting at the creepers, so Jason demanded, "Shoot! What are you doing?"

Drake swore and answered, "I think my gun's jammed. I can't get it to fire." The creepers were fifteen yards away and coming at a dead sprint.

"Now's not the time for this crap!" Jason unleashed another torrent of bullets. This round tore through the torso of another creeper. Blood oozed out of all the wounds in the beast's naked chest. It coughed, and more foamy blood splattered to the pavement. Drake was still fumbling with the jammed rifle, but he managed to take his 9 mm pistol from his belt and get off three shots. They all hit a surging creeper, who fell to the street, and the lifeless body rolled the remaining distance into the truck.

By now, there was just one creeper left, and it was the one that Jason had declared the leader of the pack. Coming at a dead sprint, it was now close enough that its bloodshot yellow eyes and the veins in its arms were dangerously visible. The creeper was only feet away. Jason attempted to get a shot off, but he wasn't fast enough, for the enormous monster jumped into the bed of the truck. Its toned and pale arms grabbed Drake and then threw him from the truck to the street pavement below. The boy hit the ground hard and lay motionless. His satchel full of supplies fell off and rolled away.

The creeper turned and slashed a skeletal hand at Jason, striking him across the jawline. Jason staggered backward, with his eyes watering from the pain. He bumped into the supply crate and fell. Letting out a savage cry, the beast jumped from the bed of the truck. It landed beside Drake, who was lying on his back with his eyes closed. He'd dropped his pistol and was left with the jammed AK-47. All Jason could do was watch in horror as the creeper crawled toward his stunned brother on all fours. He cried out in an attempt to warn Drake, but his younger brother didn't respond.

Hopelessly, Jason regained his balance and moved toward the creeper, knowing that he was already too late. The savage jaws were only inches away from Drake's exposed neck. Soon, it would all be over, and Jason would be on his own in the world. He raised his gun and aimed it at the creeper, but he never got a shot off.

Drake's eyes flew open. He was staring face-to-face with the creeper, looking into the sunken face, yellow eyes, and an open mouth full of sharp fangs. He moved unbelievably fast, catching the beast off guard. Jason saw his brother reach into his jacket and extract his hunting knife. In one fluid motion, Drake took the eight-inch blade and shoved the entire thing into the creeper. The knife disappeared in the area between the creeper's neck and collar bone. The beast wailed as a fountain of blood erupted into the air. Then it reeled backward and clawed at its wound with both hands. This meant it didn't have a free arm to block Drake's next attack. The boy was already on his feet, swinging his rifle upward by the barrel so the butt crashed into the creeper's head. A sickening sound was made as the skull shattered, and more blood oozed from the wound. The beast staggered and collapsed.

Jason swore and jumped from the truck down to where his brother stood with his hands on his knees, panting. "You're such an idiot! We never should have attacked those things. You could've been bitten, and I really don't want to be left on my own." His heart was still racing, and his anger wasn't helping the cause.

Coughing, Drake dismissed the barrage of comments by saying, "It was my idea to attack them, but keep in mind that you complied." He picked up his satchel that he'd lost during the fight and kicked the dead body of a creeper at his feet. "And now there are nine less of these out there. You should be happy."

"This isn't the place to argue. We better head home, and we can talk once we're safe." Jason took the FAL from the harness on his back and handed it to Drake. "And take this. It can be used for more than a club."

Drake took the new rifle and put the jammed AK-47 in his harness. The boys began to walk down the street, armed with rifles and new supplies. With a full stash of food and supplies, they headed home. Behind the brothers was a messy, bloody street full of dead creepers, yet they would never believe what lay ahead of them.

CHAPTER 3

The walk to their apartment building was taken even more cautiously than usual, given that the gunfire in the street had alerted all the nearby creepers to the brothers' location. They didn't speak much, partly because they were trying to be stealthy and partly because Jason was still mad at himself for listening to his younger brother. He knew that it had been a bad idea to attack the creepers in such an impromptu fashion, and his mistake of giving in had almost gotten his brother killed.

As he walked beside Drake, Jason imagined what his life would be like without his younger brother. On several occasions, Drake had saved his life. The two brothers' companionship was what kept each other going sometimes. Given the dire circumstances, serious depression could come in waves. It was in these times of depression that the brothers were there for each other, neither one stopping until their sibling pulled through.

They'd been walking for quite some time, covering the distance of almost two miles, when the building they lived in became visible. Now Jason and Drake broke into a jog and ran toward it.

Before the Space Virus, the Bennett brothers lived with their mother and father in an apartment. After the plague had struck, they had been homeless for almost a year, living wherever they could find a bed and a door that locked. The constant search for shelter had led to many unwanted creeper attacks as the brothers had ventured into dark buildings. One day, it had been jointly decided that they would find a permanent residence, and that's when Jason had discovered the Happy Lane Hotel.

The Happy Lane was in central downtown New York. Jason had spotted it one day while they were hunting for a house. The most appealing aspect of the hotel was that an exterior fire escape led all the way to the penthouse suite. This meant the brothers could get all the way to the roof without having to go inside. Naturally, Jason had decided to live in the penthouse, so the brothers had broken into the penthouse and spent about three months stealing tools from local hardware stores to change all of the locks. It had been Jason's idea to reinforce the doors with steel plates, and that had been accomplished by using scrap metal from the many abandoned cars. Eventually, the penthouse suite had been turned into a safe haven. It was the only place that the brothers felt protected from the creepers.

Jason had already begun mounting the fire escape stairwell when Drake spoke, "Listen, I'm sorry about earlier. I never should have tried to convince you to attack the creepers."

Not wanting to discuss the topic any further, Jason cut Drake off, "Hey, don't worry about it. I'm only mad at myself for putting our lives in danger. However, you were completely right about what you said. We need a change. I'm tired of living like we do."

Now Drake was smiling. "You mean it? Do you have any plans on how we'll change our situation?" They were halfway up the stairwell.

"Well, there's only one thing that I can think of." Jason began fishing for the keys to the apartment out of his dirty cargo pants. "It's just like you said. I think we have to go to Miami. If there actually are people there, then maybe we're not alone in this world after all." Topping the stairs, Jason began using the five different keys on his keychain to unlock the five deadbolts in the door.

"Really?" Drake sounded incredibly happy. "We can actually go to Miami? How are we going to get there?" He was talking impressively fast, and Jason was struggling to keep up with what was said.

"Just calm down. We'll have to talk about all of that later. First, let's just get inside. I'm super hungry, so we can discuss this at dinner."

Prevailing in unlocking the final deadbolt, Jason pushed the heavy door to the penthouse open and stepped inside. Drake followed into the dark suite. Seeing as the electricity had shut off over four years ago, the only light in the apartment was coming around the steel bars that they had welded into the frames of the windows. They'd also use candles for light too, but

37

Jason insisted on extinguishing them anytime they were out to reduce the risk of burning their safe house down.

The penthouse suite was enormous. It had eight rooms, including an enormous kitchen. The brothers kept the kitchen stocked as much as possible. Unfortunately, despite the many kitchen devices, the only way they could heat food was the fireplace. It was originally gas-powered, but Jason had modified it to burn wood. The suite also had four useless televisions.

Drake sat his satchel full of canned goods and the loaf of bread on the kitchen table. Jason followed, and together, the boys began sorting and putting the food away in the different cabinets. Through the barred windows, the sun was visible, slanting down behind the enormous skyscrapers of the Big Apple.

After organizing the food for a few minutes, Jason began planning what he'd fix for their dinner. Drake lit the fireplace while his brother took a pan from underneath the useless stove. He opened a can of green beans with a manual can opener and then dumped the contents into the pan. Next, he opened a can of smoked sausages and began slicing them into the green beans. He stirred up the mixture and then put the pan in the fireplace to warm.

"I'll set the table," Drake volunteered. This was a sign that he still felt bad about what he'd done.

"Thanks," Jason replied. He took two paper plates from the cabinet and some plastic forks from a jar. This was how they ate every day. With no running water, the brothers tried to reduce the need for cleaning. They'd take sponge baths using the same bucket of soapy water every day for a week. The times had certainly changed, but the Bennett boys had managed to adjust. Sadly, it seemed they were the only ones.

After five minutes of direct flame, Jason took the pan from the fireplace. The green beans-and-sausage combination was warm, so he scooped the mixture out onto the two paper plates. Drake took one, and together, they sat down at the overly fancy dining room table and began eating.

The boys ate in silence for a couple minutes until Drake prompted, "You said that we could talk about going to Miami while we ate dinner."

Jason took a bite of sausage and chewed thoughtfully. He swallowed and responded, "Well, as I see it, that might be our only chance of surviving the virus. We can't continue living like this forever."

It was beginning to get dark, so Drake finished his food and began to light candles around the kitchen and dining room. He replied, "I completely agree, but how are we going to get to Miami? That's quite a trip."

"Well, we certainly can't get there on foot." Jason took another bite of his dinner and helped light candles. "It seems our only choice is to find a vehicle that still works."

"Can you drive?" Drake looked at one of the barred windows.

Jason shook his head. "No, but surely it can't be that hard to learn. The only problem will be getting the gas to take us all the way to Miami." He took a thoughtful bite of the green bean mixture.

Drake frowned at this. "I hadn't thought about that. What are we going to do? Have you come up with anything?"

"I'm not positive that it will work, but our best bet is finding a long tube or something and then using it to siphon gasoline from nearby vehicles after we find the one that we want. We could fill the tank here in New York City and then stop along the way and refill when we need to get more fuel."

"That is such a great idea!" Drake truly seemed enthusiastic. "I bet it will work."

"It has to work. We won't have any other options." Jason's tone was grim. He sat in silence for a moment, considering the situation. Finally, he began helping his brother with the task of cleaning the table. After the task was complete, he said, "We should probably get some sleep because tomorrow sounds like it will be an eventful day."

Drake argued, "It's only eight o'clock, and I'm not tired at all!" He threw himself down on the sofa in the living room and picked up an outdated magazine to read by candlelight.

Sighing, Jason said, "All right, be in bed before ten. I'm going to sleep right now. Good night."

"Good night," Drake replied. "And tomorrow is going to be a success. I promise it will."

Jason took one of the candles from the table and walked down the hallway, leaving his brother on the sofa. The penthouse suite had two bedrooms, and Jason walked to his. He went inside, placed the candle on his nightstand, and sat his weaponry—an AK-47, two pistols, three knifes, and a hand grenade—on his dresser. Then he changed into a brand new white T-shirt out of a package and some new shorts after he removed the tags. Given the situation and the difficulty of washing clothes, the brothers found it easier to just take clothing from stores during the day. They were always wearing new things. The only articles of clothing that they wore repeatedly were the gun harnesses on their backs and pistol holsters on their belts.

After changing, Jason brushed his teeth without water. He looked in the mirror above his sink. A weathered, hard face stared back. It wasn't the face that should belong to an eighteen-year-old boy. His eyes had lost their youthful twinkle. He could have sworn that they used to be a much brighter blue, but now, they just seemed gray. His long dark hair had lost its shine, but this was probably because Jason hadn't seen a bottle of shampoo or conditioner in some three or four years.

Jason spit foamy toothpaste into the sink one last time and then went to his bed. He extinguished the candle on his nightstand, and the room became completely black. At first, this had taken some time to get used to, but now Jason was accustomed to sleeping in complete darkness. He lay back into his pillow and closed his eyes, trying to clear his mind of the plans he had made for the next day. In only minutes, the exhausted boy fell asleep.

It was the same recurring nightmare that Jason had experienced many times before. In the dream, it was the middle of the night, and he was being shaken awake. He sat bolt upright in bed and found his father and mother standing in his bedroom.

His father spoke, "The creepers have made it into our apartment building. They will probably be in our room soon. We don't have much time." Jason now noticed the shotgun in his father's hand.

Mrs. Bennett continued in a hushed but frightened tone, "Go quickly and wake up your brother. We will have to fight to survive."

Jason rubbed his eyes and stood quickly. In the dream, he was thirteen years old, and his brother had just turned eleven. He quickly ventured down the hallway of the apartment he and his family lived in at the time the dream took place. He opened the door to his brother's room and went inside. In the distance, he heard a crashing sound. Jason quickly walked to Drake's bed and shook his younger brother. Drake immediately stirred. "What's wrong?"

"It's finally happened. The creepers are here." There was another crash that came from the direction of the living room. Jason's mom screamed, and a gunshot sounded.

"My gosh! What do we do?" Tears suddenly started to well up in Drake's eyes. He was young and scared with no idea of what he should do. At this age, he was completely dependent on Jason and his parents.

Jason took Drake by the hand. In truth, he was utterly terrified too. Yet he tried his hardest not to show it for the sake of his brother. Neither one of the boys had a weapon as they crept into the hallway.

The brothers stopped immediately when a hissing sound came from the living room. This was the first time they had ever heard a creeper from such a close distance. Another gunshot was fired, and Jason's dad yelled, "Leave her alone!"

Jason ran forward, with his brother following behind him. Turning the corner from the hallway, they ran into the living room, which revealed a terrifying scene: Mr. Bennett was standing in the middle of the room, holding his shotgun. His wife cowered behind him. There were three creepers in the room, and they had probably entered through the front door, which had been torn off of its hinges. The beasts were terrifyingly muscular, with pale skin and piercing yellow eyes. One of them was growling, with its thin lips pulled back to reveal wickedly sharp teeth.

Drake called, "Daddy!" He looked like he was about to run to his father, but Jason pulled him back.

Mr. Bennett pulled the trigger, and a creeper dropped, the shotgun pellets piercing its body in a multitude of places. Jason had never seen this much blood. He didn't have much time to look though, as four more creepers stormed into the room. A feeling of hopelessness was omnipresent now. Mr. Bennett called out, "Run, boys! Deborah, go with them. I will hold these things back for as long as possible."

His wife hesitated. "I can't leave you alone. The boys will need all the time that they can get." The creepers were moving closer to the Bennett parents.

"Jason and Drake, I know that this is hard for you to hear, but you've got to run," yelled Mr. Bennett as he fired once more and injured another creeper. Jason stood motionless and could do nothing but watch in horror as two more creepers stormed into the apartment. Somewhere deep down, he knew that it was over, but he couldn't give up hope and abandon his parents.

Jason couldn't listen to his father's instructions. "I won't leave you! I can't."

As her husband shot another round into the creepers, Mrs. Bennett yelled, "Jason, listen to your father! You've got to do this. This is the only way you'll survive. Run." Tears were running down Jason's face now. He was crying just like his brother, but still, their tears were no match for the tears of their mother. She was bawling like an infant as the creepers closed in.

In hindsight, to this day, Jason wished that he would have listened. He should have just taken his brother and ran. Instead, he had refused, and what he saw next would haunt his dreams forever. With over ten creepers in the room, Mr. Bennett couldn't hold them all off. He shot many rounds into the multitude, but in a split second, one of the monsters dove forward and knocked him off of his feet. His wife cried out, but that was no good. The creeper was on top of him. He tried to push the beast off of him, but the creeper's strength was far superior. It savagely sank its teeth in Mr. Bennett's shoulder. He howled out in pain and then fell silent and limp.

This was the last Jason or Drake saw of their father. The boys turned and ran down the hallway, toward the fire escape. The pained cries of Mrs. Bennett were enough to inform the boys that she too had been attacked and bitten.

Jason and Drake continued down the hallway. The sound of snarling creepers followed closely behind. They rounded a corner and saw the fire escape only yards ahead.

Jason screamed, "Run!" Jaws were gnashing behind him. He had never been more afraid in his life.

Drake threw the fire escape doors open, and the brothers sprinted outside. They turned and began to dash down the stairs together. Now Jason had the time to see there was just one creeper in pursuit. Its expressionless face and sunken yellow eyes were only yards away. The beast was taller, faster, and stronger. There was absolutely no way that it wouldn't catch them unless a miracle occurred. Jason couldn't help but throw up his hands and yell out, "No! Stay away!"

The dream was brought to a quick halt when Jason awoke. His eyes snapped open, and he found himself sitting up in his bed and mumbling, "No!" He was sweating all over. He sighed upon realizing that the entire thing had been a dream, but he still couldn't wipe the memory from his mind. This was the worst of his many repeating nightmares. He always hated remembering the night he lost his parents and his home, and reliving it in a dream was even worse. Afraid to go back to sleep, Jason silently lay in his bed, with his blanket pulled up to his chin. Outside the whooping and shrieking of creepers was very loud. He stayed motionless in the pitch-black room and listened to it while waiting for the sun to slowly rise.

CHAPTER 4

The morning took a long time to arrive. Jason lay in his bed for what seemed like days, yet sleep evaded him completely. Eventually, the rays of sunlight that slanted around the steel bars in his window alerted him that it was time to get up. He crawled out of his bed and ventured into the bathroom, where he combed his disheveled hair and brushed his teeth. He walked back into his bedroom, where he stuffed his pockets with ammunition, put his handgun in its holster, and strapped the AK-47 assault rifle to his back.

By the time Jason had made it into the living room of the apartment, his brother was already waiting for him. Drake wore a gray jacket over a white V-neck shirt with black jeans. He also had his rifle, pistol, and the long military knife that he always carried. Drake asked, "How did you sleep?"

"I didn't."

This wasn't an uncommon response, so Drake continued, "Are you ready to go find a car?" A nervous smile flickered across the younger brother's face.

Jason asked, "Do you want to eat first?"

"I already did." Drake picked up an empty can of preserved peaches from the coffee table, showing it to his brother. "Here is yours." He handed Jason a similar opened jar with a spoon poking out of the top.

"Thanks," Jason took the jar and began to quickly eat it. "I have no idea how long it will be before we eat again. Do you think that we should take any food with us?"

Drake shook his head, "Nah, even if we find a car, we can still come back to our apartment to pack for the trip to Miami. It shouldn't take more than four or five hours if we're lucky."

At this time, Jason finished the halved peaches and threw away the can. "Then let's get out there! Surely one of these cars still works."

The two brothers went out of the apartment. Jason took the time to lock every single deadbolt before following Drake down the fire escape. They walked swiftly and quietly, not being brave enough to make much noise before they checked to make sure the area was clear. Over the years, they had come to learn that fewer creepers were out during the early morning and evening. They tended to be out much more frequently during midday and in the middle of the night. Therefore, the brothers would try to be out at the times the creepers were not as active.

After dismounting from the winding flights of fire escape stairs, Jason and Drake crept to the street. Both boys had their rifles in their arms in case they were to become necessary. The boys gingerly made their way to the street but stopped immediately when Drake held up his hand. They crouched down behind a large truck.

Jason silently whispered, "What?"

"I heard something move. It was over there." Drake pointed to indicate the noise had come from the far side.

"Are you sure? I never heard anything." Jason had barely finished the sentence when a scraping sound became audible from where Drake had pointed. "All right, cover me. I'll go check it out." He began slinking around the truck so as to get a clear view of the source of the sound. Suddenly and unexpectedly, there was a flapping sound, and a crow took off from on the street.

"Oh," muttered Drake as he watched the large bird disappear behind one of the many skyscrapers. "That wasn't a good start to the day of car shopping."

"Well, it could have been worse. That could have been a creeper."

Drake argued, "Well, didn't they use to say that black birds are unlucky?"

"I'm fairly certain that was cats. Now, c'mon. The way is clear." They stood up, facing the truck they had hid behind. "Let's start here." Jason tugged on the handle of the truck's door but turned away in a discouraged way. "It's locked."

Drake peered down Broadway Street. As far as the eye could see were cars pulled to the side of the road. He remembered how all the people had tried to flee the Big Apple, thinking that it was the source of the "plague." Most of them never made it, and the mass exodus had led to numerous traffic jams and thousands of murders on the streets. When put in a situation of sheer panic, most of the people had completely fallen apart. In order to escape and protect their wives or children, some men had gone as far as killing anyone in their way, be that a complete stranger or their best friend. It had been the darkest time on earth. The memories often made Drake wonder if creepers or if humans were more monstrous. Still, the complete solitude made the brothers long for other human companions.

Jason led Drake down the street. They continually tried to open the car doors, but to no avail. A few would open, but none of them had keys in the ignition. After about fifteen attempts, Jason said, "I never thought that it would be this hard to find a car."

They continued walking, when suddenly Drake called, "Lamborghini!" He took off in a jog, running to the bright red sports car thirty yards away. "This thing is beautiful!" He pulled on the handle, and it opened easily. "Thank you, God!"

Drake crawled in and examined the interior of the fancy sports car closer. There was fine leather, the dashboard was very intricate, and the steering wheel was arguably the most beautiful thing the boy had seen in his life. He muttered, "I think I'm in love."

That was before he spotted the body. The first thing he saw was the skull. It was sporting empty eye sockets and rotten skin. There was a substantially large hole in the skull, and the pistol in the corpse's hand told the rest of the story. Drake was out of the car faster than he had gotten into it.

"What happened?" Studying the look on his brother's face, Jason asked, "What did you see?"

"There was a body. It was rotten and nasty. Someone had killed himself in that Lambo, so let's just find something a little less freaky."

Jason nodded and said, "I completely agree." Still armed, they ventured further down the street, only stopping at other cars on the way.

Another fifteen minutes with no excitement, and things were beginning to look hopeless. Drake had ventured off to the other side of the street, leaving Jason alone but not out of range. A modern silver minivan parked beside a flower shop caught Jason's eye. He walked to it and opened the door without a problem. Things began to look even brighter when he spotted a car key innocently laying in the driver's seat.

"Hey, Drake, come here."

The sound of shoes slapping the pavement grew louder as Drake ran over to where Jason stood. "Did you find something?"

Jason, who was already in the minivan, replied, "Let's not hold our breaths." He took the key, stuck it into the ignition, and then turned it cautiously. The engine roared to life.

Studying the dashboard, he said, "It looks like I'm not going anywhere. We don't have much gas." Jason killed the engine and then crawled down to the pavement. He slid the key into his jeans pocket.

Drake was obviously excited. A childish grin was spreading across his face. "You said that we were going to siphon gas from the nearby cars, right? What will we use to do it?"

Standing beside the minivan, Jason bit his lip. He was looking at his brother, but then he spotted the building behind Drake. "There's a flower shop right there. I could go in there and probably find a garden hose. I think those can siphon if you cut the ends off of them."

"That's a brilliant idea! I'm coming too."

Drake began to follow his brother toward the flower shop, but Jason turned around and said, "No, you need to stay here with the van. We've made enough noise that I wouldn't be surprised if the creepers show up. I need you here to keep watch and alert me if any come, got it?"

Drake had learned not to argue much with his older brother, so he reluctantly went back to the minivan and got inside, shutting the door behind him. Finding this suitable, Jason then headed toward the flower shop. The door was locked, so with his gun raised, he kicked the door in.

The interior of the shop was dark, but the sunlight shining through the large glass windows helped to illuminate some of it. The air was heavy and musty, which wasn't a surprise because of the amount of dead potted plants and bags of potting soil in the back of the store. Taking a deep breath, Jason slowly advanced. He had his pistol in his hand just in case there were creepers in the building. This was the kind of place that they seemed to live in during the day.

The shop was fairly empty. He stumbled around, searching for a garden hose in the dark, but he didn't find one. He explored the main body of the store before spotting a closet door in the back. He walked toward it, looking side to side and scanning the store for a garden hose. Not seeing one, Jason cautiously opened the door to the closet. He was surprised not to come face-to-face with a creeper. Jason walked into the dark and mysterious room. It was a supply closet that seemed surprisingly empty. Remembering a flashlight that was clipped to his belt, Jason took it and illuminated the small room. The light revealed three whitewashed shelves built on the opposite wall. Other than a few pots for plants and a bag of potting soil, the closet was empty. Discouraged, Jason turned and walked back into the heart of the store.

Then he heard the gunshots.

The sudden chatter of gun fire pierced the silence. He instantly knew where it was coming from, and he broke into a sprint. The gunfire could only mean one dreadful thing—creepers had arrived.

Throwing open the door of the flower shop, the sight that met Jason was horrifying. His brother was standing on top of the minivan. He was clutching his AK-47 and shooting rapidly into a large pack of creepers only forty yards down the street. It was definitely among the largest groups of the monstrous beasts that Jason had ever seen; he counted at least sixteen. They were running in a full-out sprint, with bloodshot eyes purposefully locked onto Drake, who obviously couldn't fight all of them off.

Jason swore and took his AK-47 from the harness on his back. Immediately opening fire into the group of creepers, he killed two of the beasts in almost no time.

Still, that was not enough to slow the assault. They were closing in far too quickly to all be fought off in time.

More gunfire chattered, and Jason yelled, "Get in the van, Drake!"

Drake, who couldn't understand what his brother had said, looked confused while continually firing rounds into the pack of creepers. His shots were very accurate. He fired a bullet that ripped through the neck of the creeper leading the pack. Blood spewed into the air, and the monster howled before dropping to the ground, tripping two additional creepers who were following closely behind.

Once again, Jason yelled, "Drake, get in the van!"

This time, Drake seemed to understand. After firing several more shots for good measure, he jumped down from on top of the van and threw the driver's door open. He leapt inside. From twenty yards away, Jason watched as his brother shut himself inside and locked the doors. Seconds later, the creepers hit the van at full speed. They lowered their shoulders and plowed into the vehicle, which rocked violently but survived the contact without anything more than a few dents.

On Jason's count, there were twelve creepers remaining, all of which were hissing and snarling at the locked van. They peered through the window at Drake, but the beasts weren't smart enough to figure out how to get to him. Drake clutched his rifle and gazed back with uncertainty as they began to slam fists and claws into the van. Jason still had the car key in his pocket, so his brother was stranded.

Jason had frozen in place, panicked and unsure of what he should do to save his brother. One of the creepers jumped onto the hood of the van and then kicked into the windshield, which burst into a spiderweb of cracks. Knowing it was now or never, Jason opened fire from in front of the flower shop. The first few shots killed the creeper standing on the van. As that one fell, the others turned in unison to face Jason. Eleven pair of hungry and hate-filled eyes locked onto the eldest Bennett brother.

After swearing under his breath, Jason cupped both hands and held them to his mouth. He yelled, "C'mon! Leave the van alone and come get me!" Then taking his rifle again, Jason shot two more creepers. The wounded collapsed, but the others came barreling forward. He turned feverishly and ran back into the flower shop. He slammed the door muttering, "I probably should have thought this through."

Through the large windows in the front of the shop, the creepers were visible getting progressively closer. Jason turned and ran into the depths of the store, trying to come up with a plan of attack. Nothing came, and his thought pattern was disrupted by the sound of glass breaking. A creeper had jumped through one of the windows, which had shattered and lacerated the monster terribly. The creeper, who was covered with bleeding wounds, advanced slowly toward Jason. In an attempt to conserve ammunition, he picked up a flower pot and chucked it, striking the creeper in the temple and sending it to its knees. A quickly fired bullet killed the creeper instantly.

He looked from the dead body up to see the rest of the pack of creepers following him into the flowershop through the shattered window. There were far too many for Jason to fight, so he had to run. Hoping for the best, Jason bolted along the back wall of the store. Despite the darkness, he found exactly what he was looking for—a backdoor. The sound of footfall was closing in as he tried to open the door that was his only chance of survival. To his relief, the door swung open, and Jason ran through it.

The initial brightness of the sunlight faded, and the reality of what was going to happen to him came sinking in. Jason was in a long narrow alley that extended to both his left and right. There were no places to hide, nothing to climb, and no apparent way to escape. His only option was to run, but the creepers were faster and would catch him for sure. Still, he took off. His shoes slapped the ground as he sprinted forward, splitting puddles left behind from a recent storm. He was running faster than he ever had before. Creepers followed him into the alley, growling and slashing the air with their claws.

By now, Jason was halfway down the alley, and he saw a street ahead. The creepers were gaining ground; he could swear he could feel the hot breath of one on the back of his neck. He wanted to scream, but no sound escaped his mouth. Everything was over. Jason had fought the apocalypse for five years just to be killed alone in an alley by a pack of creepers. He felt a claw slash his back, shredding his shirt. He whimpered in pain but continued forward. Jason knew he was going to die.

Suddenly, from the street in front of him came a jaw-dropping surprise. There was a blaze of lights and a sound that had become a distant memory—the squeal of tires. A large black truck had sped down the street and stopped abruptly. The sound of a car horn blared out, and for a second the creepers stopped in confusion. Jason was confused too, but he continued forward. In the bed of the truck stood Drake, gun raised. He opened fire on the creepers that were pursuing his brother. The driver's side window rolled down, and an arm clutching a pistol reached out. The gun went off several times, and three creepers dropped.

A man leaned out of the window. Jason didn't get a good look at the man, but he heard a shout, "Jump in the bed of the truck!" He did as instructed, leaping up to the truck. Drake grabbed him and pulled him to safety. The truck's driver yelled, "Hold on!" The vehicle lurched forward down the street. It was an unfamiliar feeling for both brothers as they sped away from the astonished creepers.

After a brief pause, the boys began shooting at the beasts, but they didn't hit any from the back of the moving vehicle. Neither of the brothers knew where they were heading, but anywhere seemed better than among the creepers. The truck veered from the street onto Broadway and then began picking up speed. More creepers emerged from alleys and within buildings. They were apparently drawn out by the noise.

"This is more creepers than I've ever seen in my life," yelled Drake. He was barely audible over the wind whipping past.

"I agree!"

By now, there must have been fifty of the monsters outside on the street to watch the action. All of them stared on as the truck barreled down Broadway and headed out of New York. With the creepers growing smaller in the distance, Jason and Drake sat down in the bed of the truck. The only choice they had was to wait and see where they were going, but they knew nothing could be worse than what they had just escaped. For now, they were just enjoying the ride.

CHAPTER 5

I t had been so long since either Drake or Jason had ridden in a vehicle that neither of them remembered what it felt like. As they sat in the bed of the mysterious black truck and watched the angry creepers shrinking farther away, questions swam in both of the brothers' heads.

Drake broke the awkward silence. "Any idea where we are going?"

Still watching the creepers disappearing in the distance, Jason replied, "I have absolutely no idea."

The truck sped forward, swerving around some of the cars that had been abandoned in the middle of the street. Jason looked at the Happy Lane Hotel as they passed it. He and his brother had spent months trying to make the penthouse safe to live in. Now, as they were leaving it behind, he had the feeling that he'd never see the apartment again.

Drake studied the cracked pavement whizzing by. "Should we try to jump?"

"No." Jason shook his head. "We would probably be killed on impact."

"Well, that might be better than going to an unknown place with a complete stranger."

Jason interjected, "Keep in mind that this complete stranger saved us. He can't be completely horrible. And yesterday, you were complaining about how you missed people. Well, this is the first human we've seen in three years!"

Drake nodded and moved from a crouching position to sitting down because the wind had become too strong. "Then I guess we will have to just see where we're going." He had the AK-47 clutched in his hands, but now, he put it in the harness on his back.

With the creepers out of sight, Jason also strapped his rifle to his back and sat down by Drake. He took a deep breath as if he was about to speak, but he said nothing. The two brothers didn't know what to do. The truck had traveled far enough from the Happy Lane Hotel that the walk back would be potentially fatal, especially considering darkness was soon to fall. On the other hand, neither Jason nor Drake knew where the man driving the truck, their apparent savior, was taking them.

"I guess we should ride this out," said Jason. "See where we're going. We might as well relax."

By now, the tall skyscrapers of New York City were growing distant. The truck was on the outskirts of the enormous city. Decrepit, empty shells of buildings appeared to be shrinking into the horizon. It had been many years since the Bennett brothers had been outside of New York City. In the time that had passed, the area had changed into an entirely new world. The highway had cracked, and tall shoots of grass and vegetation grew through the faults in the pavement. In the distance, Jason could see an overpass bridge that had crumbled and fallen. They drove past the remnants of a gas station that appeared to have burned down at some point. This area had become unrecognizable since humanity had fallen.

After riding in the bed of the truck for another half hour, the scenery completely changed again. They had traveled into a far more forested area that was thick with nature and wildlife. The truck had veered from the highway and started to wind down a gravel road nearly five minutes ago. Both of the boys had completely lost their sense of direction and become solely absorbed in the winding road and dense forest.

"This is amazing," breathed Jason. He was barely audible over the hum of the engine. The trees' leaves were a various shade of red, yellow, and orange. He couldn't remember ever seeing so many different colors of foliage. In a matter of minutes, skyscrapers had been replaced with enormous trees. The metropolitan jungle had given way to a living forest.

"What is that?" Drake was pointing in the direction the truck was driving. Jason looked, and what he saw came as a surprise. In the middle of the forest stood a small wooden house. The house was old and in rather poor condition, but the smoke rolling out of the chimney showed that it was probably in use.

The truck rolled to a stop in front of the woodland house. Both boys jumped out of the bed quickly. Upon landing, they clutched their rifles and pointed them at the driver's side door as it swung open. The mysterious driver stepped out very slowly, eyeing the Bennett brothers. They returned the glare and took in all the details regarding the appearance of their rescuer. The man was probably in his midthirties. He had dark hair that draped over his shoulders in an unkempt fashion. The man wore a necklace that showed off a jagged animal fang. He wore a cut-off camouflage jacket and dark military-grade pants. A lit cigarette was perched between the man's lips, and sunglasses with reflective lenses were sitting on his nose.

The silence was broken when the man spoke, "So are you going to shoot me? That's hardly fair, seeing as I just saved your lives from those creepers."

Jason faltered but eventually lowered his rifle. Drake did the same. This man *had* saved them, but over time, the boys had grown accustomed to trusting no one. "Sorry," Jason mumbled. He then took a deep breath and slowly stated, "I'm Jason Bennett, and this is my brother, Drake."

The man ran his eyes over both of the brothers, evaluating them and seeming to take in every detail. He spoke again in a much softer voice, "Well, it is nice to meet you. You can call me Fox." He spat on the ground between his boots then asked, "How old are you boys?"

"I'm eighteen," Jason answered.

"And I'm sixteen." Drake's voice was quiet.

Fox nodded. "Interesting," he said. "You are both so young. I don't remember when I was that age, but I know that I hadn't been through all of the hell that you have."

"So you know what we've been through?"

"I think that I have a pretty good idea," Fox said. "And I applaud you for being able to survive all of this time in New York City. I am anxious to learn a little about your past."

Jason and his brother exchanged a quizzical look. Neither of them could sense any impending danger, so they harnessed their rifles. Jason asked, "Could you tell me why you saved us back in New York? We were certainly going to be killed."

"We have nothing but time, boys. Let's go in for a cup of tea before we continue this conversation. You do drink tea, correct?" Without waiting for a response, Fox turned and headed toward his house. The brothers followed. Jason made a mental note that the keys were left in the ignition of Fox's truck.

Drake whispered, "Should we go in the house?"

Jason cautiously nodded after he decided this mysterious man might be a very useful ally. It had been so long since he had experienced contact with another human being apart from his brother that he felt socially awkward. Nevertheless, Jason began to follow Fox across the colorful leaf-blanketed ground. Drake followed closely behind, with his hand resting on the hilt of his knife.

As they walked, Jason broke the imposing silence of the forest by asking, "So do you see many creepers out here?"

Fox spat again and answered, "Maybe once a week or so, but not as much as I'm sure you boys did."

Drake finally spoke again, gaining more trust in Fox. "Why do you say that?"

"Well, before the apocalypse, there wasn't too many people who lived out here. The population that became infected has nearly died off. It only makes sense that New York City would have more creepers because there was a higher preapocalypse population. Every time I go into New York City for supplies, I am amazed by the number of creepers still left."

By this time, Fox and the brothers had stepped onto the creaky porch of the house. Fox took an iron key from within his camouflage jacket and used it to unlock the old-fashioned deadbolt built into the front door. He forcibly pushed on the door with his shoulder, and it reluctantly swung open.

"Welcome to my home," said Fox with a discernible amount of pride. "I know it isn't much, but it has been everything I needed."

The brothers followed Fox into the dimly lit house. Despite the rather unimpressive outward appearance, the interior of the house was roomy and felt welcoming. They had walked into a living room, which had a sofa and two armchairs arranged opposite a fire in the hearth.

Jason pointed to a travel bag that was packed and sitting on the couch. It was stuffed with what appeared to be clothes and cans of food. "Are you planning on going somewhere, Fox?"

Fox had already walked through the living room. He said, "Actually, I am. We can talk about that while I'm brewing tea. Are you boys hungry?"

"Yes," answered the brothers in unison. They followed Fox through the room. It was lit only by the flames from the fireplace, which danced wildly and cast suspicious shadows through the living room that put the unaccustomed boys on edge. The brothers rounded a corner after Fox and stepped into a much brighter kitchen. Afternoon sunlight peeked in through a round window. Against the far wall, underneath the window, was a pantry; one door was open to reveal stacks of food packages and cans. There was a small stove attached to a propane tank nearby.

Fox reached out and turned the stove on, and to Jason's astonishment, a flame flickered to life. He pointed toward the flame, searching for the right words to say. Fox only nodded and said, "Yes, I have propane. I actually get it at the same place I get gas for my truck. I wanted to find a generator for electricity, but I never managed to do that."

Drake smiled and said, "It would have been nice to have propane in our safe house."

"Yeah," continued his brother. "We were cooking everything in the fireplace."

Fox began to dig through the pantry. "Would you eat some soup?" He took out several cans of various soup flavors and then sat them in front of the brothers. "Please, take your pick."

Both of the boys selected a can of soup and handed it to Fox, replying, "Thank you so much." He opened the cans and emptied them into two pots, which he sat on burners on the stove. He took another pot and filled it with water from a large jug, putting this on a different burner. Then he took two teabags from the pantry, which he sat in the water so the tea would begin the process of brewing.

Turning to Jason, Fox said, "I think we need to talk." He walked across the kitchen and sat down at a small card table that had two other seats, which he motioned to. Jason wondered what the point of the two extra chairs had been, but he decided against asking.

The brothers sat down, and Jason asked, "Sure, what's up?"

"I was just kind of hoping you could tell me about your past. You boys are amazing. I have no idea how you managed to survive as long as you have. I was thinking that we could work together and share what we know about the creepers." Fox had now taken a hunting knife from his belt and was using it to pick dirt from underneath his fingernails.

"That's a very good idea," said Drake. He was obviously growing far more comfortable around Fox. "You should start."

The conversation carried on for several minutes while the food cooked and tea brewed. The men learned a few secrets from each other, but for the most part, their idea of creepers was the same. Both the brothers and Fox knew the virus could only be spread through biting. They knew creepers came out more at night for hunting. And most importantly, they knew how to kill a creeper. The boys learned that Fox got his gasoline from an operating station in New York City, and they learned he made a monthly run into the Big Apple to gather supplies, which is how he had ended up finding and saving them.

At last, Fox stood up and walked back into the kitchen. The tea was finished, so he poured it into three drinking glasses and put the soup in two mugs. A cup of tea and a mug of soup were set in front of both brothers, who gratefully began eating. Fox sat down opposite them and said, "You asked about where I was going. I have decided I trust you both, and I'm willing to share." With two pairs of eyes on him, Fox reached into his jacket and took out a piece of parchment. He sat it on the table and opened it, showing the Bennetts.

Drake read aloud, "Miami, Florida."

"Yes," Fox replied. "I found this inside one of the supply crates in New York City. "I think that there is a settlement there, and that is who's been delivering all of the crates."

Jason had already taken a folded piece of paper from his pocket. He sat it in front of Fox.

"You have one too?" Fox asked the question after reading the parchment.

Jason answered, "Yes. We had discussed the situation and decided that we were going to attempt traveling to Miami. We were trying to find a vehicle to take when the creepers attacked, and then you showed up just a little later."

"Well, I see." Fox scratched his chin. His blank face seemed to conceal what he was thinking. "I was planning on attempting to travel to Miami myself. I have grown tired with how things are going, and I'm seeking change."

"So what should we do?"

"I have one suggestion." Fox paused, trying to figure out how to express the next statement. "I am leaving for Miami in the morning," he began. "I will take you back to your safe house. If you want, you can stay there. Or if you want to, you can gather your gear and accompany me on my journey to Florida."

The brothers exchanged a long look. They could read each other's expression. After seconds of quiet, Jason finally spoke, "If we were both going to Miami, our odds would be so much better if we went together. Plus, I like you. You seem trustworthy, and I think we will make great allies."

Fox looked to Drake. "What about you? Are you in too?"

Drake nodded. "I completely agree with my brother. Let's go to Miami."

Fox, a smile on his face and a twinkle in his eyes, stuck out his hand and shook each of the brother's hands in turn. "Welcome aboard. Now eat well, for we have a long journey ahead!"

CHAPTER 6

Jason woke up to rays of sunlight shining through the window of his room and onto the bedspread near his feet. He sat bolt upright, then paused for a moment as he remembered where he was. His brother lay beside him, still very much asleep. "Hey." He shook his brother. "Wake up!"

Drake sat bolt upright. A knife had appeared in his hand from underneath his pillow, and he waved it in the air. "Back, get back!" Blinking a look of revelation as he came out of a deep sleep, Drake hid the weapon and said, "Oh, sorry, Jason. That's a habit."

Jason, thankful he didn't lose a limb or finger, mumbled, "I knew I should've slept on the couch."

"How late is it?" Drake had the feeling of being in an unfamiliar room and not knowing where a clock was. He looked around but didn't see one.

"I think it's getting late," replied his brother. "The sun is getting really bright."

Both boys rolled out of bed, gathered their weapons, and headed into the kitchen. Fox was sitting at the card table. He was balancing his time between eating a plate

68

of scrambled eggs and playing a game of solitaire. He looked up. "Good morning, boys. Are you ready for the big day?"

"Yeah," said Drake. "And where did you get the scrambled eggs?"

"Well, I had two hens," said Fox. The oven beeped, and he stood up.

"You *had* two hens? How old are the eggs?"

Walking across the kitchen, Fox said, "I actually gathered them fresh this morning." He opened the beeping oven and took out a large tray on which sat two whole chickens that were cooked to a golden-brown perfection. Pointing at the chicken on the right and then the left, Fox said, "Boys, meet Sally and Susan." A puzzled look crossed his face as he looked closely at the cooked hens. "Or maybe Susan and Sally."

Jason asked, "You cooked your pet chickens?"

Fox, bagging up the birds for later, answered, "Yeah, it's a shame I don't have a dog because they are much larger." He looked up to see the expressions of horror on the brothers' faces. "Relax, I'm only kidding."

Relieved, Jason asked, "So are we still sticking with the plan from last night?"

"Yes."

The plan that Fox and the brothers had come up with was simple if they avoided any major run-ins with creepers. The brothers had decided that there was no need to return to their safe house because there wasn't anything there that they needed. Fox had a great supply of food, medical supplies, and weapons already loaded into the bed of his truck. Additionally, six ten-gallon metal tanks had been loaded into the back of the truck. Fox was going to take the boys into New York City one last time so that they could go to the operating gas station he had found and fill the tanks with gasoline. Sixty gallons should be more than enough to get to Miami.

For the next fifteen minutes, Jason, Drake, and Fox carried on pleasant conversation while the brothers ate oatmeal. They loaded all of their weapons and then gathered a few additional items of provision, including an atlas and the bag of baked chickens, before heading out.

Fox stopped on the front porch of his house for a second. His eyes were sad as he affectionately rubbed a board on the railing of the porch. He spoke to his old home, "Thank you. You've been good for me for a very long time, and I hope I can make it back here and see you again." He paused as if allowing memories to swirl inside his head. Then, blinking back a tear, Fox looked to the boys and asked, "Are you ready to hit the road?"

"Definitely," they replied together. The brothers and Fox walked to the truck and got inside. Fox ran his eyes over his prized home one last time and then started the engine. The truck turned around and began to roll down the driveway. The bumpy gravel road made the metal fuel tanks bounce in the bed of the truck. Inside the cab was one long bench seat. Fox was driving, and Jason sat in the passenger seat with Drake between them. The truck rolled forward in silence.

The trip from Fox's house to the gas station was just over half an hour. Conversation was limited, but Jason was contented to sit back and watch Fox drive.

Jason was eighteen, yet he had never driven before. He watched Fox in fascination as he shifted gears, steered, and performed other basic driving actions. Fox noticed Jason watching and said, "Want me to teach you how to drive?"

"That might be a good idea. You'll probably need some relief at some point during this trip."

"You're right," replied Fox. "The hardest part of driving was worrying about other drivers, and that's no longer a problem."

The next few miles were spent with Fox demonstrating various functions of his truck and explaining the basics of driving. Jason watched and tried to remember everything that Fox instructed. He was developing what he felt was a basic understanding of the skill when Fox said, "This is it." He steered the truck across three lanes and into a gas station parking lot.

The gas station was old and painted a light green. The pavement of the parking lot was fairly cracked, and six abandoned cars were scattered around. Fox swerved his truck around an old cab and purposefully parked by a gas pump. He seemed as if he'd done this many times.

As soon as the truck was in park, Fox began giving more instructions, "All right, the truck undoubtedly attracted further attention. I hope it was not too much, but the occasional creeper shows up when I'm getting gas. You two will cover me while I fill the tanks. It will take a while." He threw the driver's side door open and got out, taking his wallet out.

Jason questioned, "Why do you have a wallet?"

Fox opened the wallet and took out at least twenty one-hundred dollar bills. "Back in the day, this would be really valuable." He paused, flashing the handful of money in the air. "Still, the machines don't know otherwise." He fed the first of the bills into the gas pump, punched a button, and then began to pump gasoline into the tanks in the back of the truck.

"How do the pumps work without electricity?"

Fox smiled and said, "I found the only solar-powered gas station in the state."

Things were quiet for several minutes. Half of the tanks were full before the first of the creepers arrived. It came in solitude, stumbling from side to side like a rabid dog, until it spotted the boys. The whole character of the beast suddenly changed, and it began to spit and hiss. Without warning, it charged, but it was only able to advance mere feet before both Bennett brothers landed equally fatal shots—one in the head and one in the chest. The creeper fell.

Fox applauded. "Nice shooting, boys, and now for the real test."

"What do you mean?"

"Look," Fox said. He pointed down the road, and Jason saw a pack of creepers sprinting toward them. There were nine in all, which was a very large group for creeper standards. "Your gunshots must have attracted their attention." The group was advancing quickly. As the boys raised their guns, Fox continued, "Only two more tanks to fill. You're going to have to fend off the creepers for about five minutes to give me time to finish filling them and then my truck."

The boys opened fire without any hesitation. They dropped four creepers almost immediately, spilling a large pool of blood onto the New York City streets. Still, there were five more of the monsters left. By this time, Fox had pulled his revolving pistol and began opening fire. Soon, the three of them had managed to kill all of the remaining creepers. Fox proved to be a great marksman as well, downing two creepers with four shots.

Two quiet minutes passed before the gas pump shut off. "Now I need to fill the truck." Fox began filling it after paying just over three hundred dollars for the fuel in the tanks. The familiar hissing of creepers once again became audible in the distance.

Jason glanced down the street to see another group of creepers. This one was smaller than the first. The group hadn't seen Fox or the brothers yet. He pointed at the creepers in the distance and held a finger to his lips. Drake and Fox both looked in the direction he was pointing and then they too saw the creepers. All three of them raised their weapons and steadily took aim. The element of surprise was on their side.

Everything changed in mere seconds. Drake yelled out, "Jason!"

Startled, Jason lowered his AK-47 and demanded, "What?" The sudden outburst had attracted the attention of the group of creepers, which began charging toward the boys.

"Behind you!" The warning didn't come in near enough time. Jason tried to turn around, but before he could, he was struck from behind by enough force that he swore he'd been hit by a car. Having no time to tense his muscles because the impact was unexpected, Jason's body was bent limply and thrown to the asphalt below. He turned as he fell so as to see his attacker, which was a creeper who'd apparently managed to sneak up behind all three humans while avoiding detection. Jason's skin felt like it was being peeled off as he slid across the driveway. He cried out in pain as he skidded to a stop, but he had to quickly regain composure as the attacking creeper threw itself on top of him.

Fox opened fire at the first group that Jason had spotted while Drake was trying to get a clean shot at the creeper on his brother. Jason was on his back, and the creeper was bent over on top of him. It lashed out with its mouth in an attempt to bite him on the neck. He was still clutching his AK, so he turned it and rammed the creeper in the head with the butt of the rifle. There was a sickening crack, and Jason was certain that he should have killed the monster, but the blow from his gun barely slowed the creeper at all.

Fox had killed two of the distant creepers and continued to shoot at the rest after exchanging his revolver for a 9 mm handgun of some type. Drake was still nervously fingering the trigger of his rifle. His brother and the creeper were tangled together, exchanging blows and rolling around on the ground in a potentially fatal wrestling match. Drake knew he couldn't let his brother be bitten, but the constant movement made it impossible to take a clean shot without risking hitting Jason.

From on the ground, Jason felt the slash of three sharp claws shred his shirt and cut his stomach. The cuts weren't deep, but they stung terribly. With his rifle, he once again smashed the creeper in the face and then took his hunting knife from his belt and impaled it into the beast's stomach. He didn't even have the time to pull the knife out before a clawed hand slapped him across the face. Jason kicked and managed to roll over so that he was on top of the creeper. Staying clear of the virus-spreading mouth, Jason began to punch the creeper in the skull. He felt a dent that had been left by the butt of his rifle just above the creeper's left eye.

"That's the last of them," Fox announced as he finished off the group of creepers he'd been shooting at. He glanced from the brawl on the ground to Drake, and then back to the brawl, muttering, "You're not gonna get a clean shot." With that, Fox was off, scurrying toward Jason. He had a machete strapped to his back that he preferred for close-range conflicts. He unsheathed it now and moved in closer to the fight. He was acting quickly so that Jason wouldn't be bitten, but nothing was guaranteed.

Jason was rolled again, with the creeper on top now. The struggle continued. The beast gnashed its teeth and leaned into Jason, who was pressing against it with his rifle. He eventually managed to get his right leg out from underneath the creeper. He pulled back and then kicked outward, striking the creeper in the chest. The force of the kick threw the monster backward. Gunfire rang out, and two bullets pierced the creeper's side. Jason watched Fox, who had snuck up behind the creeper, swing his machete at the beast. The sharp twenty-inch blade passed through the creeper's neck without much resistance. The beast's head tumbled to the ground, and the body followed suit. A stream of blood began running across the pavement from the monster's neck.

Jason lay back onto the ground for a brief second before rolling over and pushing himself to his feet. Fox patted the boy on the back and said, "Nice work. That was way too close."

Drake ran over and gave his brother a hug. "We better get this bandaged up." He pointed to the three scratches on Jason's stomach.

"Good idea," said Jason. He looked at both his brother and Fox. "And thank you. You both saved me. I was so close to being bitten."

"Well, what are friends for?" Fox patted Jason's shoulder affectionately. "Now, let's go, I'm hoping to make it through Washington DC and to Charlotte for the night."

"That sounds like a plan," said Jason. "I've never been to the capital before." He and Drake followed Fox across the bloody parking lot. They stepped over the decapitated creeper and got inside the truck, which pulled away quickly before any more creepers could arrive. Both the tanks and truck were full of gas now. Five minutes later, the brothers were leaving their home, New York City, and they both knew that they'd never see it again.

CHAPTER 7

"Boys, welcome to Charlotte." Through the front windshield of Fox's truck lay the empty shell of a city that seemed to glow in the dying light of the setting sun. Large abandoned skyscrapers stretched into the sky, which had changed to different colors of pink and orange.

The trip had been made successfully and easily, with hardly any creepers interfering. They had passed through Washington DC very quickly, only stopping to investigate a mysterious crate in the wild and over-grown front lawn of the White House, which had also been consumed by vegetation such as moss and ivy. The crate was, just as they had guessed, another supply crate identical to the ones dropped in New York. They'd pried off the lid, on which the words *Miami, Florida*, had been stamped in black ink. Because of the discovery of the supply crate, the brothers had decided that there must be crates dropped off to some of the larger cities and not just New York. This had provided hope that there were even more people out there somewhere.

The trip from DC to Charlotte was made fairly quickly and safely; the most dangerous part of the journey was the segment that Jason drove. Fortunately, he was a quick learner and had figured out enough so that he was driving reasonably safely after an hour or so time. The group had conversed throughout the entire trip too. Jason and Drake shared some of their background, and Fox did the same. They learned that the rough and ragged man had once been a high school world history teacher. The bond between Jason, Drake, and Fox strengthened as they traveled and visited. The brothers had laughed more at Fox's witty sense of humor during the trip than they'd laughed in the past few years combined.

As the truck rolled into Charlotte, from behind the steering wheel Fox said, "This used to be a great place back in the day. My sister lived here with her husband. He was a marine. She was pregnant when the Space Virus got to her. Her husband was overseas at a rescue mission in Australia. I'm not sure what became of him." Fox looked sad briefly. He blinked several times.

"Well," Jason started, but neither he nor his brother knew what they should say. "I'm very sorry about your sister."

"Yeah," agreed Drake. "That's a very sad story."

Fox turned from the road they'd been driving on for the past hour and a half. "Yeah, thanks. We are going to make a quick pit stop though."

Drake asked, "Where are you taking us?"

"We are going to go by my sister's apartment. There is something there that I really want to pick up. It might come in useful too. I've been wanting to do this for a while, and since we're here, it needs to be done."

Inquisitive now, Jason asked, "Well, what are we going to pick up?"

Fox reached up and turned his headlights off so as not to be noticed by any more creepers. Smiling, he answered Jason with only, "Now that's part of the surprise. You can't ruin all my fun." The truck turned again, and he pointed to a tall brick building. "That's her apartment. I'm sure of it. If you want, we can stay there for the night."

"That sounds good," Drake said. "I didn't want to sleep in the truck."

The truck continued forward. Fox asked, "Where are all of the creepers?" They hadn't seen one in Charlotte yet, which was somehow ominous in its own way. Finally, they arrived at the apartment building. Fox turned into the parking lot and killed the truck's engine. He checked his harness to make sure he had his machete, checked both pistols, and then asked, "Are your weapons ready, boys? We'll probably encounter some creepers inside here."

"I'm ready," both boys said at the same time. They unharnessed their rifles and got out of the truck on one side; Fox, on the other. The three met around the front of the truck and crept toward the silent apartment building that loomed ahead.

The surrounding skyscrapers and other large buildings blocked out the light of the setting sun. The street was very dark by now, which was something that Fox and the Bennetts could use to their advantage. It had rained recently, and water had puddled up in the cracks and low spots of the parking lot asphalt. The front entrance of the apartment building was visible ahead. Fox led the way, silently advancing toward the door. He stopped outside and put a finger to his lip and pressed his ear against the door. He remained listening for several seconds and then said, "I can hear them in there. From the best I can tell, there are three."

Drake asked, "Are you serious? You can actually tell how many there are in there?"

Fox nodded. He grabbed his pistol in his left hand and took his machete in his right hand. "Get ready. Stay close behind." With that, he lowered his shoulder and rammed into the door. It creaked very loudly as it swung inward, revealing a dark and large lobby that Fox entered without any hesitation. Jason and Drake stepped in right behind him. Across the dark room, the silhouettes of three creepers were visible. They were hard to see but definitely there. Snarling came from the beasts. Fox groaned. "Oh, just shut up." He took one of his pistols and shot twice. Two of the creepers howled in rage but then collapsed after the fatal shots pierced their torsos.

"Nice shot!" Jason and Drake prepared to take down the last of the creepers, but Fox objected.

"Don't shoot him. Watch this." Fox reared back, bringing his machete behind him and preparing to throw it. At the same time, the creeper charged in a flash of sharp fangs and yellow eyes. He threw the machete, and it spun hilt over blade through the air until making contact. The blade impaled itself right in the center of the creeper's forehead. The throw couldn't have been any more accurate or perfect. The stunned mutant grabbed at the hilt of the machete piercing through its skull. A wide-eyed look of surprise spread across its face as if it had just realized the inevitable fate that was to come, and then it fell to the ground in a dead heap.

"That was awesome! How on earth did you do that?" Jason watched in fascination as Fox walked over to the creeper and forced his blade out of its skull. The machete was covered in blood that Fox wiped off on an armchair in the lobby before sheathing the weapon.

Finally, Fox answered, "Well, I practiced that for a long time at my house. I found the perfect target—a big oak tree—and started throwing my knife enough that I eventually killed the tree. It takes accuracy and power to kill a creeper with a machete."

Jason replied, "Yeah, their skulls are so hard! Yet you pierced it like it was a piece of cardboard. That was very impressive."

Fox smiled. His white teeth glowed in the dim light of the room. "What can I say? I have an arm." He winked and turned. "Now, c'mon. Let's get up to my sister's apartment and find a place to crash for the night. I don't know about you boys, but I'm tired."

"It's been a long day," agreed Drake. "I'm definitively ready to catch a little sleep. Will we be safe in her room?"

"We can lock the door, and I think we'll be just fine."

Fox took a flashlight from his belt and led the boys up a winding staircase that was occupied by rats, spiders, and bats, but no creepers. Once they reached the third floor, he led the way down a dark hallway. Dusty paintings hung from the walls of the corridor that had been abandoned quite some time ago.

After going halfway down the corridor, Fox stopped and pushed an apartment door open. He stepped inside, looked around, and then declared, "This is it. C'mon."

The boys followed into the room. Drake closed the door and locked it behind him. Looking around, the apartment seemed undisturbed. It looked as if it could have been abandoned only days before. There were two beds, which were both unmade, a bathroom door that was closed, and window blinds that were open. A view of the bright moon that was hanging over downtown Charlotte was visible. A thin layer of dust covered everything in the room.

Fox rummaged through drawers and shelves for a little while. He eventually had found four candles that he lit, along with a lantern that had been on a nightstand beside one of the beds. The warm glow of candle light illuminated the room almost entirely.

"Now it feels a little bit more homey." Fox smiled then continued, "I bet you're anxious to see what I dragged you all the way up here for, right?"

Jason nodded. "The suspense is killing me."

"Better suspense than creepers," teased Fox. He then walked to the bed on which the brothers were sitting and handed them a dusty picture frame.

"A picture? That's what you brought us here for?" Drake tried to not sound entirely disappointed, but his attempt failed.

"Don't be ridiculous. Just look at the picture." Drake wiped a thick layer of dust from the picture frame and studied it closely. In the picture, a beautiful dark-haired woman was smiling and hugging a tall man wearing a camouflage military uniform and clutching a long black rifle. Fox pointed to the woman. "That is—um, *was*—my sister." He pointed to the man with the rifle. "That's James Holder, my brother-in-law." He pointed one last time. "And most importantly, this is James's rifle. He was a marine sniper, and the last I had heard from my sister was that he'd left one of his sniper rifles in this room to be used as protection. We're going to take it. That will come in extremely useful."

Jason stood up and asked, "So where are we going to find this weapon? Do you have any idea where we should start searching?"

"Well, I have a pretty good idea." Fox walked across the room and to his sister's closet. He opened the door and began to rummage through the clothes hanging from a rack and small drawers that were built into the bottom of the closet.

Drake questioned, "Need us to start looking in here?"

Fox smiled broadly and pushed the hanging clothes to one side of the closet, revealing a safe built into the wall. "No, I think I got it." He examined the safe and then swore. "It's locked. I need a four-digit code."

"Try a year," suggested Jason. "When was your sister born?"

Fox punched in the four-digit code into the safe and tried to open it. Nothing happened.

Drake now spoke up, "What about a date? Is there some significant event in your sister's life?"

"Well, I can try her birthday, listing the date, month, and then last two digits of the year." Fox punched another code into the safe, and once again, nothing happened.

Jason exclaimed, "Wait!" Fox turned around questioningly. "When were they married?"

Fox thought for a second and said, "I actually know this because it was on Valentine's Day."

Picturing the numbers in his head, Jason said, "Try 0-2-1-4. That's February fourteenth."

Fox keyed in the numbers, and once again, nothing happened. Drake said, "Wait, this is the husband's safe, isn't it?"

"Yes."

"Well, if he was in the marines, then he'd probably use the international date system, listing day before month. Try 1-4-0-2."

Fox entered the code, and the safe swung open. He grinned and said, "I'm very impressed, boys." Then Fox leaned down to peer inside. "Here it is." He reached inside the tall safe and took out a very long rifle with an enormous scope mounted on the top. The black rifle glistened magnificently in the candlelight that filled the room.

"Now that is a beautiful gun," Jason murmured, mesmerized by the sleek body of the rifle and its beautiful craftsmanship.

Fox carried the sniper rifle to the window of the apartment and began toying with the scope. He adjusted several complicated-looking knobs before holding it to his eye and saying, "Oh, there we go." The gun was then pressed into Jason's hands, and Fox said, "Take a look out the window."

"Really? It's night."

"Just do it."

Jason put the rifle to his eye and peered out the window. What he saw completely amazed him. The rifle had been equipped with a thermal scope that represented heat readings as different colors. Cooler temperatures were shown as shades of blue, and warmer temperatures were represented as shades of yellow, orange, and red. Bright yellow dots were visible at over a mile away, and Jason instantly knew that these dots of heat were creepers.

Drake took the sniper rifle next. He gasped. "This is so cool!" He moved the rifle around the window and then pulled it into the room. He then swung the rifle around the entire room, studying the interior. Focusing the scope on a picture frame mounted on the wall, he said, "That picture frame is dark blue." He then saw a vase. "That looks cool too." He turned the rifle further around the room and then froze, pointing the rifle at the bathroom. A startled expression crossed his face.

Fox said, "What's wrong?"

Handing the rifle to Fox, Drake whispered, "There are three creepers in our bathroom."

"Really?" Fox took the gun and held it to his eye. Through the thermal imaging scope, he could see the very distinct outline of three creepers, and they were upright but motionless behind the closed bathroom door. Now he whispered, "I think that they're asleep."

They looked at each other uneasily, contemplating the situation. Finally, Jason asked, "What should we do?"

Fox smirked. "Well, we could try out this rifle." He raised the rifle and pointed it. "Get your guns ready, boys. I'm gonna shoot one of the creepers through the wall, and the other two will probably come out, so you boys need to cut them down."

"Okay," the brothers answered in unison.

"So are you ready?"

"Yeah."

Fox raised the large weapon. He held it firmly yet delicately and aimed it. He took a deep breath and then exhaled slowly. The gun went off, louder than any single gunshot that the brothers had heard before. The bullet tore through the wall, and the scream of a creeper came from within the bathroom. The bathroom door was torn from its hinges, and two angry creepers leapt out.

Jason and Drake opened fire. Their bullets tore holes through the first of the two monsters in hardly any time. The dying beast lashed out toward Fox but collapsed to the ground before it reached him. The other creeper, however, sprinted across the room untouched and slashed a clawed hand toward Fox. Fox ducked the blow and responded by lashing his foot out; his heel caught the beast square in the chest. The creeper stumbled back, giving Jason a clear shot. He aimed his rifle quickly and fired, but the creeper once again lunged forward, and the spray of bullets sailed over its hideous head.

As the creeper approached, Fox swung the sniper rifle like a club and struck the beast in the skull. It howled furiously and kicked out. The creeper's foot struck Fox in the shin, and he stumbled backward and fell to the ground. The creeper, standing above him, hissed its approval. Moving quickly, Fox grabbed the machete from his back and threw it toward the creeper. The creeper dodged the spinning blade, and it bounced off the wall behind him. With a look of anger in its eyes, the creeper picked up the machete from the floor behind it. Jason and Drake launched another round of bullets that tore into the side of the creeper, and it staggered.

"Nice shooting, boys," Fox chirped from on the ground. He watched the dying creeper. "I thought it was going to get me." He was interrupted by a growl. The wounded creeper, machete in hand, snarled at Fox as it dropped to its knees. Fox watched, expecting the beast to collapse to the ground at any given moment. Instead, the wounded beast refused to drop. It reared back and threw the machete from across the room. The weapon spiraled through the air toward Fox, who was initially surprised by the sudden effort but then attempted to roll out of the path of the spinning blade. The effort was not enough. The dying creeper watched with a triumphant smile as the blade pierced Fox's stomach, and then the monster toppled to the ground, dead.

Suffocating silence hung in the room. Jason couldn't believe what had just happened, and it had occurred so quickly. "Fox!" He ran toward his fallen friend. A stain of blood was already spreading across his shirt. "What are we going to do?" He looked toward his younger brother for advice, but Drake said nothing.

Fox set the sniper rifle down beside him and grabbed the hilt of the machete that was impaled in his stomach. A look of disbelief spread across his face, and his mouth opened. His breathing was becoming raspy, and his voice was nothing more than a whisper, "Well, that is unfortunate." He reached behind him to touch the pointed tip of the machete that was jutting out of his back. Tears formed in his eyes, and he looked into Jason's eyes apologetically, "Jason, I'm sorry. I shouldn't have brought you two into this."

Drake was crying now, hot tears streaking down his cheeks. "This is my fault! I should've shot the creeper before it got to you. I should've…" His voice faded, and he tucked his face into the crevice of his arm.

Jason took charge. "Drake, stay with me. We got to get him out of here."

A hazy look had spread across Fox's face. He said, "It's no good. Don't worry about me. Get out of here. I enjoyed our time together." With that, Fox closed his eyes and fell back, collapsing on the ground.

CHAPTER 8

Drake led the way down the dark staircase. Jason followed closely behind, with Fox leaning against him for support. The machete was still impaled in his stomach, and he was fighting to remain conscious. He groaned and whimpered every time he went down a step.

"Please," moaned Fox. "Just let me die here."

"We can't do that, Fox," answered Jason. "That's not what you really want anyway, Fox. You've lived through too much to die here." Suddenly, he pointed across the dark lobby and yelled at Drake, "Creeper!"

"Got 'em," Drake fired a chain of bullets, piercing the ominous darkness. The creeper that Jason had pointed out had no chance of evading the wave of ammunition. Several of the bullets tore through the beast's stomach, and it howled. Blood spattered from its stomach and squirted across the room. Occasionally, creepers would seem to refuse to die. This one, however, dropped on the spot into a crumpled and very much dead heap.

"Nice shot," Jason said. As he and Fox reached the bottom floor, he reached inside a pocket of Fox's bloody pants and removed the car keys. He called to his brother, "Drake, come and take Fox. I'm going to go start his truck. We need to get him out of here."

Drake asked, "Where are we going?"

"I'm not sure. We need to find somewhere where we can bandage him up and stay for a while—somewhere not infested with creepers." As if on cue, the front entrance of the apartment building was thrown open, and a creeper sprinted into the lobby. Jason was caught transferring Fox from his shoulder to his brother's shoulder. He yelled, "You take Fox." Drake grabbed the injured man and then Jason pulled his handgun on the creeper. He fired the gun, and the bullets struck the creeper in the chest. It collapsed, and Jason ran past it and through the front entrance door of the building, knowing that more were probably nearby.

Being alone in the dark night made everything seem scarier, and Jason felt vulnerable. With the key to Fox's truck in his hand, he hurried across the parking lot. As he walked across the moonlit area, he could see two hideous creepers circling the truck. One was sniffing a front tire. The other creeper was standing behind the tailgate. It sniffed the air and then it peered into the bed of the truck, where the supplies were. The creeper reached into the back of the truck and removed a can of processed meat. It studied the can for a minute and then took a bite. Sharp teeth tore into the metallic can, and the creeper began to chew both can and meat. The hungry creeper seemed to nod in approval, but then it dropped the can, which bounced off of its foot and rolled underneath the truck. The creeper suddenly started hissing at the truck and trying to figure out how to get the can out from underneath it. Decisively, the monster squatted down and then grabbed the truck's bumper. Seemingly effortlessly, it picked up the rear of the truck and moved it so that the can was once again accessible. It triumphantly picked up the partial can of meat and put the entire thing in its mouth.

The second creeper was moving toward the stash of supplies. Jason knew that they couldn't afford to lose any of the medical supplies, so he had to act quickly. He had come into good range, so he raised his rifle. "Get away from my truck, now." Both creepers turned and looked at him. They charged at once, one from his left and the other from his right. Being at such close range, Jason knew that he wouldn't have time to shoot both of them. He'd have to shoot one and fight the other with his hunting knife. Thinking fast, he shot at the creeper on his right because the one on his left still had almost an entire steel can in its mouth. The one that Jason fired at was torn apart by the bullets. There was a spray of blood, and it fell, so Jason turned his attention to the other, which was only a few feet away. Jason swung his rifle at it, but the creeper ducked and then plowed into him. The two tumbled to the ground in a spiraling heap. By the time they had come in contact with the pavement, Jason was on top. He took his knife from his belt and quickly slit the creeper's throat.

Standing, Jason heard the sound of a door opening. He looked to his right to see Drake carrying Fox out of the apartment building. Fox's body hung limply in his arms. Drake yelled, "He's unconscious. We need to get him help as soon as possible! I had to leave the sniper rifle because I couldn't carry it."

"All right, I ran into a little trouble at the truck. There were two creepers." Jason hurriedly got into the truck and started the engine. The truck roared to life, and the steering wheel gently vibrated under Jason's grasp. He opened the passenger side door and called out, "C'mon, Drake!"

As Drake carried Fox toward the truck, Jason spotted a movement from somewhere down the street behind his brother. He strained against the darkness to identify the source of the movement. There was something like a wall about two hundred yards down the street. The wall was shifting and changing shapes though, constantly moving and growing closer. Suddenly, Jason could make out what it was. He swore. As it came closer, it became clearer and more distinguishable. The wall was actually an enormous line of creepers; there had to be at least thirty-five in all. They were lined up and charging down the street, faintly audible hollering and screaming their inhuman wails.

"Drake, hurry up!" Jason could not keep the urgency out of his voice. "Get Fox in the truck. We've got to go!"

Drake was about twenty yards from the truck when he stopped, having heard something. He turned his head to look behind him and saw the enormous wave of creepers. "That is not good." He picked up his pace, but having to carry a full-grown man was quite the load.

Jason put the truck in drive and held his foot on the brake. His instincts told him to get out of the truck and go to help his brother with Fox, but he knew the extra time to get back in the truck would slow down their escape. "Hurry, Drake!"

Drake was getting closer to the truck, but the creepers were only sixty yards away and coming at an all-out sprint. That translated to only seconds. Not knowing what else to do, Drake threw Fox over his shoulder and began to jog the remaining distance to the truck. His body screamed for him to stop. It burned with exhaustion and yet felt numb from the lack of sleep. Resisting the urge to surrender, Drake powered through the last few steps to the truck, set Fox down inside, and then jumped into the truck himself. He threw the passenger's door shut behind him, and subsequently, several of the oncoming creepers slammed into it. The wave of mutants was beginning to surround the truck.

"Hold on!" Jason pressed the gas pedal to the floor. Tires screeched and the truck lurched forward. The cab bounced a couple times as the truck plowed over at least three creepers that had been unlucky enough to get in the way.

Drake turned and looked out the rear window to see the enormous group that they were leaving behind. "There are so many of them." The seemingly tireless monsters still ran after the truck, but once it reached the open highway, the vehicle began outdistancing them.

As soon as the creepers were no longer a threat, Jason began giving his brother instructions. "We have to get the machete out of Fox and bandage him up so he doesn't lose any more blood." Even in the dark, it was becoming obvious that Fox's skin was growing pale. He'd lost a large amount of blood and was beginning to look more dead than alive. The truck swerved violently to the right as Jason almost ran into a bent street sign. He asked, "Now where was that switch?" Remembering the answer to his own question, Jason reached up to the dashboard and twisted a dial that turned on the truck's headlights. "There we go!"

"What should I do first?"

Examining the situation at hand while still attempting to steer the truck down the middle of the road, Jason said, "Well, the only thing I know that we should do is remove the machete." He peered at the handle of the weapon that jutted awkwardly from Fox's abdomen.

Drake looked nauseous as he studied the task at hand. "So do I just pull it out?" He sounded uneasy and uncertain. The blade was impaled entirely through Fox.

"Make sure you don't twist the machete at all. Slide it straight out." Jason looked into his brother's eyes. "C'mon, you can do this, Drake."

By now, the huge gathering of creepers were totally out of sight, and Jason had begin searching for a place to park so they could try to get Fox out of the car and into safety. Drake glanced from Fox's pale and blank face to the hilt of the machete. "What will I do once I get the machete out of him?"

"Well, the wound will be bleeding a lot, so put pressure on it until I can find somewhere to park."

Taking a deep breath, Drake grabbed the hilt of the machete. "Here goes nothing." He began to carefully slide the blade out of Fox. The truck hit a bump in the road, and the cab shook, so Drake immediately pulled his hands back. Once it steadied again, he continued slowly removing the machete from inside his friend. The blade made the sound of meat being sliced as it reluctantly slid from within Fox. After several seconds of constant pulling, the machete finally came loose, and Drake dropped it in the floorboard. He let out a sigh of relief.

"Good job," said Jason. "Now put pressure on the wound."

Drake put his hands together and covered the wound. Blood was oozing from the gaping wound, and it quickly covered his hands. Thinking fast, he tore the bloodstained shirt off of Fox's torso and tied it around his stomach very snuggly so as to suppress some of the bleeding. He said, "We need to get Fox out of here as soon as possible."

"I see a gas station up ahead. Let's park there and take Fox inside. We have some medical supplies in the back of the truck. I'll carry him inside, and you bring the supplies."

No objection came, and Jason turned into the parking lot of the gas station. He quickly parked the truck and then scanned the parking lot for any creepers that were hiding in the shadows. Seeing none, he opened the driver's side door, got out, and then ran to the other side of the truck. He reached inside and wrapped his arms underneath Fox's limp body and picked him up. Drake jumped out of the truck and then hurried to the bed, where he took out a large bag of medical supplies.

Under the darkness of nightfall, Jason carried Fox across the parking lot. The shirt that had been torn and tied around the wound was already soaked with blood, enough that the crimson liquid was dripping to the ground at periodic intervals. Soon, Drake, medical kit in hand, had caught up with him. He was holding a dark bottle of liquid and said, "I have some hydrogen peroxide here. We should pour it in the wound to prevent infection."

By now, they had approached the door of the gas station. "Good idea," acknowledged Jason. "Since I'm carrying Fox, you need to lead the way inside with the medical supplies. Be prepared for creepers though."

Drake nodded, took his pistol from its holster, and went inside with the gun raised. He danced around so that he could see the entire interior of the room and then declared, "It's clear. Bring him in."

Jason lugged Fox into the dark gas station. He was quickly growing tired from the constant weight of the unconscious man in his arms. Stepping inside the door, he sat Fox down in the floor carefully. "We have to act fast! There is no time to waste."

Drake had already uncapped the hydrogen peroxide and unwrapped the bandage. He began pouring the liquid into the wound. The peroxide began bubbling profusely. Jason took the medical supply kit from his brother and opened it. He rummaged around inside until he found some gauze and medical tape.

A groan interrupted the hunt for more supplies. Jason looked up to see Fox's eyes flutter open. He looked dazed and very weak. He struggled to form words with his mouth. "Where am I?"

Drake leaned over him. "You're in a gas station. We drove you here from the apartment building."

The hazy look hadn't gone from Fox's eyes. "Who are you two?" He stared at Jason and Drake questioningly. Jason was just about to answer when Fox let out a pained chuckle. "I'm just joking with you, boys. I'm bleeding to death, not dying of amnesia."

Jason actually smiled at the lighthearted spirit of his friend. "I promise that we're doing everything we can to prevent you from bleeding out. I don't think the stab got to any organs or major arteries." He prodded the wound enough to examine it.

Fox cursed and then mumbled, "You do realize that I can still feel that, right?"

"Sorry, but I got to do it. The pain isn't going to kill you." The bubbling had subsided now. "We need to put some gauze on the wound.

Drake did as instructed, laying the gauze right across the piercing stab mark. He held it in place with a couple pieces of tape and rolled Fox over gently. The machete had stabbed all the way through his body, and a small slice was visible in the center of his back. Blood had dried all-around it, caking onto his bare skin. Drake poured some more hydrogen peroxide into the wound and covered it with gauze. He asked his brother, "Will you help me sit Fox up?"

Jason carefully grabbed Fox from underneath his arms and then sat the man upright. Fox didn't object. His only response was a quiet groan that he attempted to suppress. Once Fox was upright, Drake began to take the medical tape and wrap it firmly around his torso so that it held both patches of gauze firmly in place.

Fox coughed. "I can barely breathe. This is horrible." He coughed some more.

"*Barely* is the key word," said Jason as he examined Drake's handiwork, of which he approved. "We need to apply as much pressure as possible to stop the bleeding."

Drake watched the gauze for a little while and then proclaimed, "I think that the bleeding is slowing! Look, Jason."

Jason directed his gaze to the gauze on Fox's stomach. It was staying white for the most part. He smiled and said, "The bleeding has definitely let up a little. I think you're going to live."

Fox swayed dizzily. "Can you lay me down? My head is swimming."

"You lost a large amount of blood," Drake replied as he helped his pale friend lie back down on the tile floor of the gas station store.

Another cough came and then Fox questioned, "Remember when I said that you should leave me in the apartment and save yourselves?" He looked Jason directly in the eyes.

Jason slowly nodded. "Yes, I remember."

"Good," said Fox. His words were sounding somewhat slurred. "Cause when I get well again, I'm going to kick both of your butts for not listening to me."

The three new friends shared a laugh inside the gas station. Outside, the world was dark, humanity was depleted, and monsters seemed to lurk behind every corner. Inside the building however, the new friends were growing closer, and for the first time, the three had found something that had been missing from their lives for a very long time—hope. Jason and Drake sat by Fox as they waited for the long night to end.

CHAPTER 9

Sleep evaded Jason. He was lying on the bed of magazines that he'd fashioned on the floor of the store. His brother slept on a similar pile of magazines right beside him. On the other side of the room, in front of the potato chip rack, Fox slept on the only two pillows that the boys had managed to find in the gas station's store. They had been sleeping like this every night that they had been in the store, which was coming up on a total of nineteen days. Finding food was easy because they were surrounded by various canned foods that the gas station had sold. By day, the brothers had taken turns between exploring Charlotte and staying to help take care of Fox, who was definitely seeing improvement.

Despite both brothers' warnings, he had started walking two days ago. He had dismissed both of the brothers' efforts to persuade him against walking with a simple, "Things aren't like they used to be. In the old world, you could take time to heal. But now, if you stay in one place for a long time, you die."

He had posed a good point, and neither of the Bennett brothers had been able to offer a successful counterargument, so they had accepted Fox's choice. He still moved very slowly and gingerly, but he was doing better than expected. Also, Fox had been drinking a lot of water and sports drinks from the coolers in the store. He said that the lost blood was being replenished and that he was feeling much better, other than the still hideous wound piercing all the way through his stomach. The wound still ached a lot, and he complained about the pain, saying that it made it sore to move or sleep.

This night, however, Fox seemed to be sleeping very well. He lay resting on his two pillows, with his two pistols setting on the ground nearby. One of his arms was stretched out toward them, and the other was wrapped around his freshly bandaged wound. A peaceful look was spread across the man's face, which was very rare when he was asleep.

Suddenly, Jason heard a scraping sound and sat upright. He looked at his brother, who still was sleeping motionlessly. Before the virus had struck, Jason would have dismissed the sound as a mouse or something of that nature. Now, however, any slight noise needed to be inspected. He reluctantly stood, taking his rifle with him. He stood still and listened for a few seconds. The noise came again. Jason swore when he could tell that the source of the noise was outside. "That's not a good sign." He crept through the dark store to look out the front window.

It was the night of a full moon. This led to great visibility but typically meant the creepers would be more active. As Jason peered through the window, his greatest fear was confirmed. There, in the parking lot of the gas station, was a group of six creepers. They walked around awkwardly and had seemed to gather around a discolored spot on the pavement that was less than ten yards from the front door of the gas station. One particularly slouched-over creeper bent down like a canine and sniffed at the spot with great persistence. Two more creepers began doing the same, sniffing the exact same area of the pavement.

"What do they smell?" Jason watched the creepers for several seconds, thinking hard. Suddenly, he remembered the night he'd carried Fox into the store. Blood had been dripping from the stab wound, and neither Jason nor his brother had thought about cleaning up the stains. Apparently, that had been a mistake because the smell of human blood had attracted the predators.

Jason was just about to sneak away from the window to wake up Fox and Drake when one of the creepers did something very unusual. After sniffing the bloodstain one last time, it stood erect and made a loud whooping noise. The other five creepers began doing the same. They sounded like six demon-possessed apes shrieking calls into the dark night. It was the scariest thing Jason had ever heard. He watched through the window as the whoops continued. He breathed the question, "What are they doing?" Soon, his question was answered. In the distance, more whooping calls answered. Through the window, Jason watched the second group of creepers, the group that had responded to the calls, emerge from the blackness of night. The procession of seven more beasts began ominously heading toward the first group. Jason was in a panic, muttering, "They're calling more creepers. They are on to us!"

He hurried across the room quickly yet quietly. He ran to Fox first, knowing the injured man would take longer to prepare for battle than his brother. Jason shook Fox firmly enough to wake him. The man sat bolt upright, clutching his stomach. He asked, "What's wrong?"

"Creepers. They found us."

"How many?"

"I counted thirteen now, but more may be coming."

Fox cursed and then slowly stood up. "What are we going to do?"

Jason, who was shaking his brother awake, answered, "We are going to need a distraction of some kind. We need something that can get the creepers off of us for enough time so that we can get to your truck and get out of here."

Drake was already on his feet, AK-47 in hand. "They've found us?" He ran to look out of the store's front window and then mumbled, "Uh-oh. There are a lot."

"What? How many of them are there now?"

Drake moved his hand, pointing and counting in his head. "I think there are twenty-two." He paused. "No, there's twenty-three."

Fox had wondered across the room and picked up something. He triumphantly declared, "This is what we need!" He held up a cigarette lighter that he had found on the clerk's counter. He tested the lighter out, and a flame flickered to life.

Jason asked, "What are we going to do with a lighter?"

"We can light a fire in here and feed it so that it will burn and create a blockade from the creepers to us. We can block the front half of the store from back here. The creepers won't be able to get to the back of the store. While they are blocked off by the fire, we can run out the backdoor and get to my truck." He stopped talking and looked at the doubtful expression on the faces of both boys. "Does anyone have any better ideas?" There was no response. "I didn't think so."

"What do we light on fire?"

Fox had already slowly set to work, lighting both Jason's and Drake's magazine beds on fire. The old papers began to burn immediately. The flames spread quickly and had soon engulfed both piles of magazines. Suddenly, there was a loud crashing sound from the front of the store.

Drake sounded terrified. "They're trying to get inside! They know we're in here."

Fox's only response was a short, "Duh."

Creepers continued to throw themselves against the store's front door. It was locked, but the great strength of the beasts would eventually be able to break through the door. It was apparent that there was not much time before the creepers would overtake the boys and Fox.

"What else will burn?" Jason looked around the room frantically. He spotted a shelf of bags of potato chips nearby that he took and dumped into the growing fire. The flames licked up the bags of crispy old chips, and they grew much taller, reaching heights of about three feet. Jason began to call out instructions to his brother, "We need more potato chips! Add that shelf over there." He pointed behind Drake at another shelf of bags of chips. Drake dumped the bags onto the raging fire and jumped backward as the flames spread quickly. More pounding on the doors came as the creepers continued to attempt breaking into the store.

Soon, the flames had jumped from the bed of magazines to a tall shelf of packaged foods. They were spreading now, so the barrier Fox had envisioned was actually taking shape. The pounding on the doors was increasing in both frequency and force.

Fox called out, "They are going to break in any second."

"You're right," Jason had to yell in order to be heard over the combination of the crackling flames and the insistent pounding on the door. "Stay here while I run and get Fox's truck. I'll bring it around the back of the store so you don't have to move very far, Fox."

Drake called to his brother as he was exiting the store through the back, "Jason! Be careful." Jason stopped and turned around, seeing the flames start climbing the walls of the store. A raging barrier flame had now formed between the creepers and Fox and Drake. Jason knew they were safe for a little while since the creepers wouldn't penetrate the flames, but he also knew that he had to hurry. "Count on it," he replied, before stepping from the heat and light of the fire into the dark and cold night. The last thing he heard was the sound of the door being torn from its hinges and the creepers beginning to flood into the store.

Outside, the night was silent and calm. All of the creepers had stormed into the store, so the parking lot of the gas station was completely empty and still. Car key in hand, Jason sprinted across the cracked and decrepit pavement toward Fox's truck. Driven by the fear for his friend's safety, he moved quicker than he ever had in his life. He reached the door of the truck, threw it open, and jumped inside. Putting the key in the ignition was difficult because nerves were causing Jason to tremble. His quaking hand eventually managed to start the truck, and he shoved the gas pedal to the floorboard. The trucks wheel's spun, and it lurched forward. It blazed across the parking lot, losing some of the supplies from the open bed as it bounced over crevices in the pavement.

Looking through a window of the store, Jason saw the creepers hissing and slashing at the barrier of flames. None of the beasts attempted to penetrate the blaze, but the flames seemed to be dwindling, and time was running low. He looked ahead again and turned the wheel enough that the truck began drifting across the parking lot. This caused more supplies to bounce out of the truck's bed. A loud metallic clatter came when one of the six fuel tanks bounced out and crashed into the asphalt. The shiny can rolled forward, and he had to swerve so as not to hit it. The can came to a stop near the back of the gas station store. After parking right behind the backdoor, Jason left the engine running, put it in park, and jumped out. He knew he'd have to help fight off the creepers so that Fox would have the adequate time to get to safety, so he hurried inside.

As soon as Jason opened the backdoor of the gas station, a wave of heat and ash rolled over him. His eyes stung, and he stepped backward, wiped them, and then charged forward. Inside, the flames had diminished, and were beginning to burn low. Two creepers were brave and jumped over them. Fox and Drake shot those two down, and from behind them Jason yelled, "Go! Run to the truck." Neither had seen him come inside. They turned around with surprised expressions. Jason continued, "Help Fox into the truck, Drake. I will hold these things off as long as possible."

Drake never objected. He grabbed Fox and helped him hurriedly walk toward the back door. Jason peered through the flames. The hissing fanged mouths and hungry yellow eyes of the twenty-one creepers on the other side returned the glare in hatred. A particularly brave creeper charged forward. It howled as it passed through the flames but seemed to not be seriously harmed. Jason gunned the monster down, but the other creepers had watched and seemed to have learned that they could pass through the flames by now. They all charged at once.

Jason wasn't prepared for the assault. He began spraying bullets into the wave of creepers that charged through the flames toward him. Some of the beasts weren't as lucky as the first had been, and their tattered clothes caught on fire. The creepers with the flaming clothing all roared and began frantically moving side to side, tripping others and knocking some down. This gave Jason just enough time to shout to his brother, "Hurry! They're coming." He kept his finger on the trigger of the AK-47 and waved it back and forth. Five creepers dropped after lucky—yet—fatal kill shots struck their vitals.

Still, there were too many creepers left. Jason refused to admit this and kept fighting as the dozen remaining beasts closed in on him. They were only yards away. One leapt forward, claws and fangs reaching out hungrily. The fatal bite was inches from Jason's right arm before he managed to strike the diving creeper in the chest with the butt of his gun. It stumbled back and tripped another beast. Jason sent lethal shots into both of the fallen monsters, but he'd already begun retreating by shuffling backward toward the exit door. Ten creepers were within arm's length. This was by far the most that he'd ever dealt with in close-range combat. All the monsters were faster and stronger than he was, so the odds of survival were very slim.

The chatter of gunfire erupted from behind him. Four creepers immediately dropped when fountains of blood erupted from their chests. Jason quickly turned to see Fox and Drake standing behind him. They'd opened fire on the creepers too, and only six of them were left now. Jason lashed out with the ball of his foot and struck a creeper in the chest. It stumbled back and fell down directly in the flames that were beginning to consume the front half of the store. Another creeper dove for his stomach with an open mouth. Not knowing what else to do, Jason shoved the barrel of his rifle into its mouth lengthwise. With a powerful chomp, the strong monster tore the metal barrel of the rifle in two with its sharp fangs. Completely weaponless and unprotected now, Jason doubled back. The creeper spit out the gun's barrel and then dove forward again. There was nowhere for Jason to go. His body tensed for the contact as the creeper soared toward him. The yellow eyes in front of him gleamed as the beast prepared to bite.

The creeper was thrown to the ground completely unexpectedly. Jason watched in amazement as Fox tackled the monster as if he'd been a professional football player. He cried out in pain as his wound faced unimaginable strain. Drake gunned down the three creepers that were in front of his brother and then turned to Fox and the final creeper who were rolling around in a struggle on the ground. He waited for a brief second, hoping for a clear shot. Jason was running toward Fox in an attempt to help, but he was too late. With a quick and powerful strike, the creeper buried its sharp fangs into Fox's shoulder. Fox swore, wrapped his arms around the creeper's head, and then jerked violently to the side. There was a sickening cracking sound as the creeper's neck snapped. It fell limply on top of Fox, who pushed it off.

"Fox!" Both brothers were screaming and running toward their fallen friend. The bite mark on his right shoulder was bleeding profusely. He took his opposite hand and held it to the fresh wound and then pulled the hand back to see blood. He stared at his bloody hand with an expression that showed unbelievable astonishment and fear, something that they had never seen on his face. He looked like he was going to cry. There were no more of the lighthearted jokes that so frequently rolled off of his tongue.

An unwelcome sound came. The roar of multiple creepers echoed from across the gas station parking lot. Jason looked through the raging flames out of the window in disbelief as what looked like another thirty creepers charged from the shadows of nearby buildings. They were bellowing battle cries and sprinting like predators toward the store, as if they somehow knew that the first wave of their kind had all been killed. The fire had spread to the majority of the building, and the entire scene was hellish.

Peering at the next onslaught of creepers, Fox mumbled, "This is unbelievable. There's so many of them. We get through the first round, but then there's more, and there's always going to be more."

Jason seized Fox and forced him to stand. "C'mon, Fox. We gotta get you out of here and get something into that nasty bite."

Drake, who was helping support their friend, offered, "I bet they have a cure for the virus in the Miami settlement! We need to get you there so you can be cured." They were walking through the backdoor now, glancing back to see the creepers getting dangerously close to the blazing store.

Jason hurriedly got into the truck and prepared for a quick getaway. Drake was leading Fox behind it. He said, "C'mon, Fox! We have to hurry. It's going to be all right! We'll find you a cure in Miami!"

Fox seemed to gain a new confidence as he stepped over the fuel tank that had fallen from the bed of his truck. He quickly accompanied Drake to the passenger's side. Drake glanced through the backdoor to see that the creepers were very near now. He climbed into the passenger's seat and turned to Fox, his hand outstretched. "I'll help you into the truck."

Blood was oozing down Fox's bare chest from his shoulder. He stared back longingly but didn't take Drake's hand. "You know that there is no hope, right?"

The new wave of creepers was nearly inside the store. Jason yelled, "There's no time for this argument! Don't lose hope on us now!"

Fox spoke softly, "I haven't lost hope for you, boys. You mean so much to me, and you gave me something I longed for—friendship." A toothy smile now spread across the man's face. "But I'm going to go out with a bang, boys."

Together, the brothers asked, "What do you mean? What are you doing?"

"I'm making a difference." Fox's confident grin flashed in the darkness. "Watch and learn! Thank you for everything you've done for me, and have fun in Miami. Now drive." He slammed the passenger door shut and stepped away from his truck.

Drake yelled, "Don't be stupid! We won't leave without you!"

As the creepers began pouring into the fiery store, Fox only replied with, "You have no choice!" Suddenly, despite both horrible wounds, he grabbed a pistol from his belt and began to run back into the store. As he ran, he let out a battle cry that was just as terrifying as anything that had ever escaped any creeper's mouth. In tears, but faced with no other choice, Jason began to drive off into the night. The last thing he saw was his gun-bearing friend grabbing the heavy ten-gallon fuel tank from the ground and lugging it inside of the store. Fox was going right at the thirty angry creepers.

Inside the store, Fox stood in the middle of the flames. They burned his legs, but he somehow never felt the pain. The horrific and ugly beasts closed in, whooping and roaring. He yelled right back, "C'mon, boys!" As the flames overtook the room, he yelled, "Welcome to hell!" The creepers were all inside the flaming store and getting nearer. Some were within arm's reach, howling their anticipation, when Fox held his pistol to the gas tank in his arm and pulled the trigger.

The explosion was enormous. Drake watched through the back window of the truck as, first, the store erupted into an enormous fireball, then the gas pumps in front of the store, and then a grand finale came when a thunderous blast tore into the silent night. The pump's large supply tank had ignited and then exploded, sending an enormous mushroom of flames, ash, smoke, and shrapnel into the air. The truck was a hundred yards away, but the flames from the blast still blazed over it. Fox had caused the explosion, and the heat, light, and flames rolling over the truck seemed like him saying good-bye one last time.

Both boys were sobbing, and their ears rung. Jason managed to choke out, "He's gone. Fox is gone." Drake nodded and sat silently, with hot tears streaming down his face. "I won't ever forget him." Hardly having anything happy in life meant that losing something that brought happiness stung even worse.

"As soon as we get to Miami, then we will tell them all about Fox so that everyone knows what he did for us."

"Yeah. Fox was a hero."

Drake, through tears, asked, "Are we going to stop somewhere?"

Thinking for a brief moment, Jason answered, "No. We are going straight to Miami. That's what Fox would've wanted." With that, the conversation ended, and the truck pushed deeper into the dark and ominous night. The smell of smoke still lingered in the air, and the memory of Fox's heroism burned in their minds.

CHAPTER 10

Drake was snoring. He sat slouched over, with his head leaning against the window of the truck and the crumpled road map resting in his lap. The boy's eyelids were puffy from crying. A steady stream of saliva ran out of his mouth. He had been very helpful in assisting Jason with getting to this point, but once Jason had an idea of how he was going to get to Miami and after they'd refilled the gas in the truck, he'd given his brother permission to take a nap.

Jason knew that Miami was very close. He could faintly see the tall figure of skyscrapers towering in the distance, so he decided to wake his brother. Shaking Drake, he gently said, "Wake up, Drake. We're almost here."

Drake sat up and opened his eyes, adjusting to the bright midday sun that hung over Florida. He asked, "How long have I been asleep?"

"About two and a half hours."

"Well, aren't you tired?"

Jason shook his head. "I'm really not tired at all. I still keep thinking about…" His voice trailed off, and he

114

changed the topic. "What do you think Miami's going to be like?" The skyscrapers were becoming slightly clearer ahead.

Drake considered that for a moment as he folded up the road map and put it on the dashboard. "I think they have electricity and running water and air conditioning and movie theatres and a water park."

Jason interrupted, "Let's be real here. I'm guessing the whole city is somehow quarantined. I just have no idea of what to expect really. Do you think they have a cure for the virus?"

"Who knows? I guess we'll just have to find out."

The road they were traveling on was filled with potholes. Jason constantly had to steer and swerve around hazards in the road. At two different times during the trip, a bridge that they'd needed to cross was collapsed, so they had had to find another route. Now he had to swerve around a fallen tree that was taking up about two-thirds of the road.

Drake suddenly said, "I really don't see any signs of life up ahead. Miami looks just like New York did—dead."

Unfortunately, Drake was right. By now, they were within half a mile of the heart of Miami, and the buildings were still dark and motionless. The street was decrepit. A billboard that appeared to show three basketball players holding rings was bleached by the sun and peeling away. The details of the buildings were clearly visible now in the bright sunlight. They had been sprayed with graffiti and many of the lower floor windows were barred. Worst of all, there was not a single person in sight.

As the truck began driving through the city streets, Jason managed to get the words out, "Where is everyone?"

"I expected this." Drake sounded like he might cry again. "There absolutely nothing here. It's just like New York City." He then unleashed a stream of foul language and lashed about violently. "I'm so tired of this! It's all over."

Jason could tell that his brother was losing hope. They drove past four abandoned cars on the side of the road and then reached an intersection. Knowing not what to say, he turned the truck in silence and began cruising down another street. A feeling of hopelessness crept over him too as they drove through more abandoned streets. Suddenly, he spotted movement in an alley to his right and abruptly stopped the truck.

Drake snapped out of his barrage of swearing and self-pity. "What was that? A creeper?" He jumped out of the truck and raised his rifle toward the alley.

"Whoa," Jason said as he got out of the truck as well so he could follow his brother. "Hold up and don't do anything stupid. If it was a creeper, then there was probably more than one, and we shouldn't go into the dark alley to pick a fight."

"Why's it matter? Do we have anything to lose? Miami was our last hope, and now even that is gone." Drake, rifle raised, was stepping closer and closer to the alley. "I just want to kill something."

"Drake, don't do this," warned Jason, but it was too late.

Peering into the darkness of the alley, Drake said, "There it is!" He opened fire, and the sound of a screaming creeper rang out. He smiled. "Got him." He began walking forward but then stopped and leaned his head to one side as if listening intently.

"What are you doing?"

"I heard something. There is more of them." Drake suddenly began backing away from the alley while keeping his gun raised and trained into the shadows.

Jason couldn't resist pointing out, "Well, I told you not to do it."

Drake was gritting his teeth. He mumbled, "I was just mad. I wanted to kill something. Life is beginning to seem pointless, so who cares if anything happens to us?"

"Well, I don't want to die today," argued Jason.

Sheepishly, Drake admitted, "Me either."

The sound of creepers was growing louder. The shadowed figures of at least ten of the beasts appeared toward the far end of the alley. They were sprinting toward Jason and Drake and letting out savage cries. Both Bennett brothers fired round after round of gunfire as they backed away abruptly. The fierce, growling monsters grew closer with every passing second. Eventually, two of them had been killed, but the constant movement and darkness of the alley made counting the exact amount remaining next to impossible.

For several seconds, the boys held their ground while firing into the pack and fending the creepers off. The battle was going decent for the brothers until Drake made a careless mistake. While jogging backward away from the alley of creepers and continually shooting at them, he tripped off of the curb and fell back to the asphalt street, landing on his back. He let out a loud yell when his head struck the street.

"C'mon, Drake," yelled Jason as the creepers emerged from the alley into the bright sunlight. "You gotta get up and help me. This isn't the time to trip or have any accidents." He aimed his rifle and took several shots that downed another creeper with three bullets to the head. A quick count still told Jason that there were six creepers left, and they were too close for him to take on by himself. "Drake!" He looked to his brother and gasped; Drake lay on the ground with his eyes closed. His rifle had rolled several feet away. He could tell that his brother was out cold from hitting his head on the street.

The remaining creepers, mouths watering and dripping saliva, were moving in on Drake's unconscious body, obviously going for the easier prey. Jason had to do something to protect his sibling. He began shooting countless bullets into the pack. The rapid fire quickly tore apart two of them, puncturing their torsos countless times. He continued firing until another two of the attacking creepers dropped, but the all-too-familiar sound of a click immediately let Jason know he was out of rifle ammunition. He threw down the rifle and began fumbling for his pistol, but he was too late. The last two creepers now loomed over Drake's unconscious body with hungry eyes and open jaws. They were lunging toward the body before Jason could even get his pistol from its holster. He watched in horror as two pair of fanged jaws came within inches of his brother's neck.

The sound of gunfire erupted from behind Jason. He watched in absolute astonishment as bullets from an unseen source ripped multiple holes in both creepers in just a matter of seconds. The unconscious Drake was saved as the two creepers who were about to make him their meal were killed instantly. Their dead bodies dropped onto him. Someone had saved him, and now his careless mistake wasn't going to cost him his life.

Jason turned around to see their mysterious savior and gasped. About sixty feet away stood a girl about his age. She was fairly short with dark brown hair and a slim tan body. She wore a white V-neck that had been torn off just below her ribcage, showing off very impressive abdominal muscles. She also wore combat pants with several pockets, all of which were bulging. It took a thick black belt to hold the slightly oversized pants to the girl's slim waist. Clipped to the belt was a pistol holster. Two knives were sheathed there as well. The girl lowered her gun and stared back at Jason.

Finally, she spoke, "It's been a while since you've seen a girl, hasn't it?"

Jason realized that he was staring open-mouthed at the mysterious girl who'd saved his brother. He lamely mumbled, "Sorry, you surprised me."

The girl began walking forward. Her gait showed that she was very athletic. She grinned mischievously at Jason and said, "You better reload your gun soon. I'd hate to have to save you again." She winked and brushed by Jason on the way to check on Drake. "Aren't you worried about your brother?"

Jason followed her, feeling so awkward in the presence of another stranger. He stepped over a dead creeper and bent down beside his brother. He said, "He'll be fine eventually. It's his own fault anyway because he tripped off of the sidewalk."

The girl laughed and said, "I have only seen you two in action once, but what I saw wasn't too impressive. You run out of ammunition, and your brother trips, hits his head, and knocks himself out."

"I guess you're right, but we've made it to this point, right?" He paused. "And how'd you know he was my brother?"

"Are you kidding me? You two are pretty much identical!" She seemed very friendly. "So what's his name?"

"His name is Drake. And by the way, my name is Jason." He scooped up his brother and began carrying him across the street to their truck. There was a visible knot on the back of his brother's head from hitting the cement. He asked the girl, "Will you pick up his rifle? And what was your name?"

The girl scooped up the AK-47 and studied it before nodding her approval. She answered, "I'm Michaela." There was a moment of silence as Jason sat his brother upright in the cab of the truck. Michaela, who was proving to be very talkative, said, "I'm seventeen years old. What about you boys?"

Jason replied, "I'm eighteen, and Jason is sixteen. He'll be seventeen really soon though." There was a moment of awkward silence as Jason stepped away from the truck and looked into the eyes of their attractive rescuer. She handed him the AK-47, and he didn't know what to say. His social skills had rapidly vanished along with society. Finally, he managed, "Well, thanks."

Michaela only smiled and teased, "Aren't you going to invite me to go with you? I just saved your brother, y'know?"

"Well, would you like to come along with us? Where were you going?"

Michaela sighed. "I lived in Orlando. There were supply crates that were occasionally dropped off, and one of them had an envelope in it. Inside the envelope was the word *Miami*. So that's when I came here to find, well, this." She sadly gestured around at the lifeless shell of a city.

Jason nodded in understanding. "Where is your car?"

"I walked," Michaela answered smoothly. Now Jason was really impressed. "So what about you boys?"

Jason looked into the truck at his brother then answered, "We are from New York City, and our story is very similar to yours. We came here after finding a supply crate with a note like yours. We had a friend named Fox, whose truck we are driving, but he was killed in Charlotte yesterday on our way here."

Immediately, Michaela looked very sad. She sniffled and apologized, "Oh, I am so sorry, Jason! That's horrible." She stepped forward, as if about to embrace the oldest Bennett brother, but realized what she was doing and stepped back, an embarrassed look spread on her face. "I'm sorry! I don't mean to make you uncomfortable. I just felt bad, and I-I was just going to hug you. I know how bad it is to lose friends. I had a dog named Tirus and—" She stopped talking and looked up into Jason's eyes.

Jason shook his head suddenly as Michaela backed away. She froze in place, and they briefly looked into each other's eyes. He stuttered, "N-no. That was nice—that you care, I mean. I haven't been hugged in forever. I'm glad you care and—"

He was cut off when Michaela threw her arms around him. He awkwardly hugged the short girl back. They remained that way for several seconds. The two had just met, but Michaela really seemed to be a caring person. He continued to hug her, unsure of when to let go. Finally, he heard his brother's voice coming from within the truck, "So I pass out, and when I wake up, you're hugging some hottie? What the heck happened?"

Michaela quickly stepped away and looked into the truck at Drake. He was rubbing the back of his head and smiling. He waved and offered, "You are way more attractive than the girls in my swimsuit magazine."

She blushed and said, "Um, thanks?"

Jason quickly intervened, "Be polite, Drake. This is Michaela, and she was the one who saved your life after you were an idiot. I told you not to go looking for a fight, and you almost got yourself killed."

Drake tried to smile and said, "Sorry, I didn't mean to be rude. It's nice to meet you, Michaela. You are very pretty." He stuck his hand out of the truck and said, "I'm Drake." She shook his hand, and he pressed, "C'mon, don't I get a hug too?"

She only winked at Jason and said, "Maybe later, Drake." She teasingly wrapped her arms around his older brother one more time before getting in the truck beside Drake.

Jason walked around and got into the driver's seat. He explained to his brother, "Michaela walked here from Orlando to find the Miami settlement just like us. I invited her to come with us."

"That sounds like a good idea to me," Drake agreed. "But where are we going?

Jason shrugged and started the engine. "I guess we can just drive around and see if we can find anything that seems useful."

The slight hint of hopelessness had crept back into Drakes' voice. "Well, what are we going to do? Miami was pretty much our last hope."

Michaela was not afraid to speak. "I have been here for one day and haven't seen anything useful, but maybe there are people somewhere."

Drake shook his head. "I doubt it. Do you see any signs of life anywhere? This whole city is dead."

The timing couldn't have been any more perfect. Jason pointed out of the windshield to the distant skyline. He sounded excited. "Look at that! What is that?" From about a mile away, shots of bright red light were visible, streaking into the sky, where they would eventually burn out.

Michael cried out, "Those are flares! Signal flares, which means someone's there and trying to get our attention.

Drake started laughing with joy and slapped Jason a high-five. This was excellent news, which neither of the brothers were accustomed to receiving.

Jason began to drive forward toward the source of the flares that still streaked into the sky. "I can't believe this," he managed. "There are people here after all. I was beginning to lose hope!"

Drake said, "I need a hot shower. It's been so long since I've had one. I'm so happy right now."

Michaela added, "I guess I found you boys at just the right time! I've waited so long for this!"

Somewhat killing the mood, Jason sighed and said, "I just wish Fox would have made it. He was so close." The joy died down in the truck, which rolled along the empty streets.

The flares seemed to be coming from the base of a large apartment building some two hundred yards away. They abruptly stopped, but Jason could already tell where he was going. As he approached the building that he believed was the source of the flares, two men became visible. Both were dressed in T-shirts and jeans and armed with powerful-looking rifles. The truck stopped in front of them, and they both smiled and waved at Jason and his company.

One man spoke very welcome words, "Hello there! Congratulations, you've made it. You are soon to be official citizens of the Miami settlement and the new United States of America. Please park your truck around the back of the building and come meet me here. I can't wait to show you around."

Jason looked to Drake and then their new friend. All three teenagers were smiling boldly. This was the first time in a very long time that any of them had felt safe. Jason asked, "What are we waiting for? Let's go see this Miami settlement."

CHAPTER 11

After parking the truck among about thirty other vehicles behind the apartment building, Michaela and the Bennett brothers walked back around to the front of the building to meet with the men standing outside. They immediately greeted Jason with a handshake and then Michaela and Drake, respectively. Of the two men, one was tall and thin while the other man was shorter and of a stockier build.

The tall man spoke first, "I'm Jeremiah Redman, and I am a soldier of the Miami settlement."

"And I am soldier Henry Osborne. It is my pleasure to meet you." This came from the stocky man. He questioned, "So what are your names and how old are you guys?"

The brothers and Michaela answered the question eagerly and then Redman asked, "So are you boys brothers?"

"Yes, sir."

He looked at Jason, Drake, and then Michaela before saying, "Well, are any of you, um, a couple or anything?"

Jason quickly spoke up, "We aren't together, but she is a new friend. We just picked her up in Miami."

"After I saved Drake's life," Michaela tossed into the conversation.

Osborne shook his head. "We've tried to get rid of most of the creepers in Miami, but that's quite a difficult task to complete. I swear those freaks are everywhere."

Redman spoke again, "I'm sure you kids have been outside for quite some time, so let's head in. You'll need to learn how things work in Miami now. We're like our own independent world. It's just a very small world."

Jason and Drake exchanged questioning looks, but they didn't object and followed Redman through the front doors of the apartment building. Osborne stayed outside on patrol. What they saw was surprising; they walked into a large blank room with white walls, white tiles, and a white ceiling. The rush of cool air-conditioning was inviting after several years without. The room had electricity too, which had become an almost forgotten luxury of the old world. The only person in sight was a tall man with dark hair dressed in a white lab coat and wearing a medical mask. He sat intently studying a stack of paperwork behind a desk that housed several complicated-looking pieces of medical equipment.

Redman said, "Before you can enter the settlement, you need a blood test with Dr. Williams here." He pointed at the doctor to whom they seemed to be walking toward. "This ensures that the Space Virus can't get into the settlement. Anytime you go out, you have to get the blood test done to get back inside, but don't worry because it is very quick and painless."

They approached Dr. Williams. He looked up from his intent study and smiled at the three teenagers. "Well, I don't believe I've seen you here." He spoke softly and kindly. "Let me test you and then you'll be free to go. Can you each hold out your right arm?" Each of them did as instructed, and Williams performed the test with some sort of cylindrical tube that none of them had ever seen. The tube was held to Jason's arm first. It pricked him and took a sample of blood. The doctor studied the tube closely and smiled. "You tested negative."

As the same procedure was performed on Drake, Jason asked, "So is it true that the Space Virus is only spread through bites?"

Williams nodded. "Yes, so far there have been no reported cases of transfer either aerially or blood-to-blood contact. We have a brilliant scientist who has been studying the virus and how it affects the hosts." Jason was going to speak, but Williams continued. "I can guess your next question though." Then he said, "Know that this test is just precautionary. I perform it just in case of a rare situation. Never once has anybody tested positive for the virus."

"Well, that is a relief," replied Jason.

After Drake and Michaela both passed the blood test, Williams instructed, "Please accompany Redman down to the settlement."

Redman smiled. "Thank you, Dr. Williams." He turned to Jason. "Now please follow me."

Jason, Drake, and Michaela all followed Redman across the large white room. They were headed in the direction of an elevator built in the wall opposite the entrance.

They walked in silence for a little ways until Drake asked, "What did that doctor mean when he said we are going *down* to the settlement?"

The group had arrived at the elevator. Redman was leading the way, but Jason walked at his side. Drake and Michaela followed closely behind. In response to Drake's question, Redman said, "Well, this apartment building has a basement. Over the past three years, the people of Miami have completely renovated the former basement into something special."

Michaela, who had been silent for the longest time since the brothers had met her, spoke again, "What do you mean?"

Redman pressed the button to call the elevator and said, "Well, the basement has been completely renovated, and we constructed tunnels to connect the basement of this building to the basements of three other surrounding buildings. It basically forms a large square of underground protection from the creepers."

An electronic two-toned beep came as the elevator door slid open, and Redman stepped inside, followed by the others. Jason was impressed with what he'd heard so far. He said, "That's amazing! How large is this, um, settlement?"

"Not too large in terms of population. There are just under five hundred people now." He paused, pushed a button on the elevator, and continued, "If you are talking in terms of size, then that's completely different. This settlement is very large. The four basements I told you about all have a different function. There are four quadrants—the merchant quadrant, the housing quadrant, the political quadrant, and the recreational quadrant. I will give you a basic tour of some of it before you are assigned an apartment."

The onslaught of new information seemed to be a whole lot to digest. In just over half an hour's time, the brothers had gone from feeling absolutely hopeless to making a new friend and being taken into a society of almost five hundred survivors. The change was overwhelming, and nobody spoke as the elevator began to sink down the shaft. The feeling of uncertainty crept back over the brothers. Everything seemed too good to be true.

Finally, the silence was broken again when Drake asked, "So, Mr. Redman, can you tell me when you arrived here in Miami? And how long has this settlement existed?"

"I was actually one of the eight people who decided to form this settlement, and that was nearly four years ago. Together, we elected a director, and we've grown a lot since then. It has taken time, but this settlement is altogether a success now."

The elevator abruptly stopped its descent, and the doors slid open. What waited outside the doors was completely astonishing to the brothers, but it was something they'd been longing to see for several years. Upon stepping out of the elevator, the world they saw was amazing. Michaela gasped, and Redman said, "Welcome to the merchant quadrant."

They had entered an enormous cement room that was air-conditioned and lit with bright lights. It was almost a forgotten sight. The room was also filled with tables, tents, and racks that all housed different goods. Some people were distributing food, some clothes, and even luxury items like DVDs and radios.

"This is amazing!" Jason turned to Redman. "How do the citizens afford to purchase these goods? What do they do to make money?"

Redman began walking forward, and the teenagers followed him. He answered the question loudly enough to be heard over the bustling people, "Well, we make supply runs once a week. A group of thirty people take trucks out to Miami and gather food and supplies from stores and homes. Since everyone physically capable participates, we have no problem with everyone taking whatever they want for free, just as long as they limit themselves fairly."

"Oh, I see." Jason thought the idea seemed like the fairest way to manage the market, and he knew that he wouldn't mind going on supply runs at all.

Heads turned and concealed stares were cast on the newcomers as they went through the market. There were hardly any people around the brothers' age. The majority of the inhabitants were middle-aged, with a few elderly people and some kids mixed in. The kids were all much younger than Jason and Drake; the oldest that Jason saw was probably twelve. Several young couples held small babies that had no doubt been born after arriving at the settlement. A few little kids pointed at Jason or Drake, surprised to see new faces in the apartment.

Redman laughed, noticing all of the attention. "It seems that you are already being noticed." He stopped in front of a table covered with loaves of fresh bread that seemed to be watched over by an elderly man with round eyeglasses and patchy gray hair. The man was hunched over a stove behind the table, and he appeared to be baking more loaves of bread. Redman handed a loaf of bread to Drake, who began to share it with Jason and Michaela. He said, "I would like you boys to meet Silas." He then spoke directly to the old man, "Silas, meet my new friends."

Silas turned around and cupped his hand around his ear before leaning forward and saying, "Heh?"

Redman shook his head. "Never mind!" He turned to the brothers and apologized, "Silas's bread is much better than his hearing. Now let's go to the housing quadrant and find you a place to live."

Together, they walked across the enormous market. The warm and fresh bread was probably the best thing that the Bennett brothers had eaten in over four years. They didn't speak much because they were too busy eating it. After walking all the way through the market, around tables and under bright tents full of clothes on racks, the group arrived at double doors that Redman led them through. The doors opened up and led into a long and narrow hallway that was decorated with several paintings that both Jason and Drake recognized.

Redman asked, "So what part are you guys from?"

Drake answered the question, "We came from New York City, and Michaela is from Orlando."

Astonishment found its way into Redman's voice. He asked, "Are you serious?"

Nodding, Drake said, "Of course. Why?"

They continued forward, but Redman had increased his pace. "This is a very big deal," he said, "You probably don't understand, but you are the first people to ever come here from out of state!"

Now Jason spoke up, "Are you serious?"

"I'm completely serious. Almost everyone here is local to Miami. Some have come from nearby cities, but nobody has come close to matching the distance that you boys traveled." He stopped talking and seemed to be thinking for a minute before asking, "Does this mean that you came here because you found the note in our supply drop?"

"Yes," Jason replied.

They seemed to be walking even faster now, matching the speed at which Redman was now talking. "This is fantastic news! It's amazing. I want you to meet with the director as soon as possible. You'll be assigned an apartment and then I'll go schedule a meeting with her. You'll have some great information that we can use, and I know we have some great information to share with you." They reached the end of the hallway, and Redman pushed through another set of double doors and held one of them open for the teenagers.

"I'm very excited about the opportunity that you are presenting us with," said Jason as he followed Redman into the second quadrant of the settlement. This quadrant appeared to have once been an enormous underground parking garage. It was square and open except for five extremely long individual structures that were all built parallel to each other and stretched almost the entire length of it. Each of the structures was painted white with green trim, and they seemed fairly inviting.

Michaela pointed at the structures and asked, "What are these?"

Redman answered, "This is the housing quadrant. Think of each of these structures as long apartment buildings. They are divided into thirty rooms each, and each room is supplied with two beds, a bathroom with a hot shower, a television, and a DVD player. They are intended to house up to four people per unit."

Jason studied the structures more closely. Large brass numbers hung on each one of them, numbering them one through five. He realized that he was holding his breath and blurted out, "This is amazing. I really can't believe all of this was built underground. This had to have taken forever."

Redman nodded as if in recollection. "It did take took a very long time, especially making the plans for everything. Construction was the easy part. This was definitely the largest underground parking garage in the entire city, and making it suitable to live in was quite a chore." He gestured with his hands for them to follow. "Now, c'mon, I'll take you to the apartment administrator, and you can be assigned a room."

He walked purposefully across the quadrant and was obviously heading to a small desk at which the stereotypical middle-aged, dark haired, bespectacled secretary sat pecking away on a computer keyboard. She seemed to be studying the monitor intently and didn't look up until Redman tapped on her desk. The woman gasped in a startled way and sat bolt upright before turning to him and apologizing, "I'm sorry, Sergeant Redman. I was very absorbed in my work."

"So I could see, Ms. Johnson." Redman chuckled. "I've got three more for you. Meet Drake, Jason, and Michaela. The boys are here all the way from New York City." He turned to the brothers. "I'm going to go talk to the director and see when she can meet with you. I'll check what apartment you boys are assigned and then come and meet you there to share what I learned." They nodded, and he quickly walked away.

Ms. Johnson smiled, pushed herself away from the keyboard, and praised, "I'm very impressed! That's an amazing trip." She looked at Michaela. "Are you three together, dear?"

Michaela glanced awkwardly at the Bennett brothers. "Well, um…" The look of uncertainty was in her eyes, and she glanced to Jason for help.

He nodded and stepped in, "Well, we just picked her up in Miami, ma'am. We really don't even know each other that well yet."

Jones smiled. "I completely understand that, so I'll make you an offer. If you three decide to room together, I will give you apartment 4M. If not, then you'll be put in two different rooms, and you'll end up rooming with strangers."

Jason looked to Drake, knowing what he was thinking. He then looked to Michaela and asked, "Would you mind sharing a room with us? It's your choice, Michaela."

She shook her head. "I wouldn't mind at all! I really like you boys." Drake discreetly fist-pumped behind her.

Jason turned to Ms. Johnson and answered, "I guess apartment 4M it is."

The secretary smiled and then handed them each a room key. She pointed and said, "Good choice. Your room is over there in that building.

"Thank you." They took the keys and left. It didn't take long to find their room. The interior was even better than any of them expected. The luxury of a functional thermostat was incredible, and the television was even better. There were no channels that actually worked, but there was a DVD player that seemed to be in great working condition. A stove and microwave were built into one of the walls. To have built the whole housing complex in three years was remarkable. Jason wondered where the supplies had even come from.

There were two beds in the room. He walked to the far one and said, "Me and my brother will take this one, and you can have the other, Michaela."

She held a hand to her heart and teased, "Aw, you are so sweet. Thanks!" She then jumped on her bed and stretched out with outspread arms. "I have missed a good bed. And TV. And a bathroom. And air-conditioning."

Drake asked, "So what do you think we should do first?" There was a rapping on the door. He called out, "Come in!"

The door swung open, and Redman walked inside with a smile on his face. He announced, "You found your room! I'm glad. What do you think of it?"

From on top of her bed, Michaela replied, "This is just amazing."

"Yeah, it's great," the brothers answered together.

"Fantastic. You can consider yourselves VIPs since you've come from New York. You boys are very important to us here, so I want to do everything I can to keep you happy." After a look around the room, Redman asked, "Do you need anything? Would you like me to accompany you to your truck to get any belongings?"

All three teenagers still had their weapons strapped on. Jason answered for himself and his brother, "We have our guns, and that's about all I need. There is some food, clothes, and medical supplies, but we can just get them tomorrow or sometime."

"And I had no supplies at all," said Michaela with a sigh. "Just me, my gun, and my clothes." She looked down at the half of the T-shirt she was wearing and then put her hand on her exposed stomach until she realized the brothers were looking at her. "What? It gets hot in Florida. I was doing good to keep my shirt on."

"Speaking of clothes," Redman interrupted, "I would highly recommend that you go to the merchant quadrant before it closes at nine o'clock. You can pick out almost anything you'd like to wear to bed or around here tomorrow. You can find any size of clothes, I promise."

"Yes, sir, count on that."

Redman turned to leave and added, "Oh, one last thing. Pick out something really nice to wear because the director would like to meet with you tomorrow at nine in the morning." He looked at Michaela. "You can come too, Michaela. Just don't get breakfast at the merchant quadrant tomorrow because you'll eat with the director. I'll be here at eight-thirty. Does that sound okay?"

"Yes," Jason answered, "That sounds fantastic. Thank you so much for everything you've done."

"None of it was a problem. It was all my pleasure." Redman stepped out the door, saying, "Now have a fun evening. Feel free to explore, and make sure you get a good night's sleep!" He closed the door.

Everything had changed so fast. Earlier that day, Jason had been mourning the death of Fox. He and his brother had been hopeless. Then his life had changed over the next couple of hours. They'd met Michaela and then been integrated into a society that had survived the apocalypse. Everything was suddenly looking bright and hopeful.

He looked around the room at his brother and new friend. "So, is anyone game to explore?"

"Let's go."

The three left the room and went out to explore their new home. Once again, a strong feeling of hope had overtaken each one of them, and given everything they had been through, any hope at all was completely welcome.

CHAPTER 12

"So how do I look, boys?" Michaela stepped out of the bathroom wearing the things she'd hand-picked at the merchant quadrant the previous evening. She was wearing a tight red dress that showed off her amazingly toned and tanned body, which was no doubt the result of spending years on the run. A pair of brown-and-silver sandals was on her feet, and she'd even gone as far as picking out some mascara from the merchant quadrant and putting some on too. She twirled around to show her attire from every angle. There was no denying that she was very pretty.

"You can't wear that," argued Jason. "You're going to make Drake and I look bad." He and his brother were wearing matching collared shirts that were a deep blue, jeans with matching black belts, and some leather shoes they'd found in the merchant quadrant after extensive searching.

Michaela laughed and smiled at Jason, teasing back, "You don't need me. You guys would look bad either way." She certainly was comfortable picking on her new friends. They hadn't known each other for more than a day, but staying up late the previous night just to converse had helped both her and the brothers feel comfortable around one another.

The entire previous night had been an adventure. After Redman left the apartments, the brothers and Michaela had gone to the merchant square to gather some supplies that seemed necessary, such as toothbrushes and hair combs, along with a set of clothing for the meeting with the director of the Miami settlement and a separate, less formal set to change into for the remainder of the day. From there, the group had returned their new belongings to their apartment before going to explore the recreational quadrant. It was impressively large too, housing half of a basketball court, an inviting swimming pool, a table tennis table, and several tables where people could sit and talk. Everything was in fairly close proximity, but the area still seemed roomy to be built in a basement. The majority of the people in the quadrant had been older, so the tables were being used more than any of the other facilities. By that time, it had been getting late, so they'd ventured back into the merchant quadrant where they'd eventually found something to eat, and then they rented a DVD from a kiosk before going to apartment 4M for the night. Together, they watched the DVD and talked enough that they were learning a lot about each other's background and then eventually went to sleep.

This morning, they had awoken at a quarter to seven and taken turns using the bathroom to get dressed. The brothers had taken about five minutes apiece while

Michaela had taken almost thirty. Now, everyone was done, and they were lying on their beds, waiting for Redman to arrive. The wait wasn't long, and at eight thirty sharp, there was a knock on the door. Through the door came, "This is Redman. I'm just checking to see if you all are ready for the meeting. Director Marinas is very excited about talking to you New Yorkers."

"Yes, we're all ready," called Jason. "Come on in."

The door swung open, and Redman entered. He too was dressed more formally today, wearing a collared shirt and khaki pants. He looked at all the teenagers and seemed impressed. He complimented, "You boys clean up very well. And you look stunning, Michaela."

"Thank you," they all answered at once.

Redman asked, "Ready to leave?"

"Yes, I think we are," responded Jason. They followed him out of the apartment, across the quadrant that was nearly empty at this time in the morning, by the secretary desk where Ms. Johnson sat in front of the computer, and then to another set of double doors that lead to a tunnel. A sign that read "Government Quadrant" hung above the double doors.

"We're going this way." Redman pushed open the doors, and the group proceeded down the hallway in silence. Eventually, he said, "I think you will really like Director Marinas. She is a great leader and one of my closest friends. There is no way our settlement would have survived without her. She was responsible for supplying us with all the materials used to construct this place through her connections with construction workers and contractors and she also proved to be an invaluable leader."

They were almost at the end of the hallway when Michaela said, "I'd imagine that running this place is a lot of work."

"Well, it is much easier now than when we were attempting to establish it. Most of what she does now is just organize supply runs. It's not like there's any serious crime because everyone is grateful to be here. When we first started, she had to organize the people and plan how to build this whole settlement." He pushed through the second pair of double doors at the end of the hallway and held one open. "She didn't do it alone. There is a board, which I am a member of, that assists, but it still took a tremendous amount of effort and meticulous planning."

"That's understandable," Jason responded as he followed Redman into the government quadrant. It was probably the smallest of all of the quadrants but still about thirty yards long and thirty yards wide. Half of the room housed a large circle of chairs that were probably for meetings, and the other half housed cubicles that looked much like a business office. Several artificial plants sat in the corners of the cement room to provide a little color. There was a door built into the opposite wall, and an armed guard stood by it.

Jason studied the out-of-place door until he was interrupted. "Director Marinas will be over here." Redman led Jason and company through the cubicles until they arrived at a particularly large one, which he walked into. Inside the cubicle was a table, and on the far side of the table sat a woman dressed in a dark purple jacket and skirt over a white shirt. She was pretty for a middle-aged woman, and her eyes seemed to gleam with intelligence. There was no doubt that this was the director of the settlement. Redman announced, "This is Jason, Drake, and Michaela." He turned and said, "This is Director Marinas."

Marinas smiled warmly and gestured to three chairs opposite her and said, "Please take a seat." She looked at Redman. "Thank you, Jeremiah. You may go."

Redman nodded and left the group alone with the director.

She said, "It's my absolute pleasure to meet you fine young men and woman. You are going to mean a lot to our settlement with your information regarding both creepers and cities on the coast." She peered out of the cubicle and said, "Oh good, here comes breakfast."

A young waitress carried an enormous tray of food in and sat it on the table. There were four fully-prepared plates on it. Each plate had scrambled eggs, toast, and small pieces of ham that had probably been canned. The waitress sat a plate in front of each of the four people and distributed silverware, drinks, and packets of salt and pepper. She asked, "Does everything look good?"

"It looks fantastic as usual, Beatrice," Marinas answered and then the waitress left. The boys began eating, but Michaela looked at the food in a puzzled way. As if reading her mind, Marinas said, "Don't worry. The eggs aren't several years old. Actually, they came from a small farm we have on the upper city—that's what we call the ghost town of Miami that is above us."

"Oh," Michaela grinned and started eating the eggs. She chewed for a second and then looked at Marinas. "These taste amazing! They are just so fantastic. You have no idea how long it's been since I've had a hot meal."

"I'm glad that you are enjoying the food with me." To Jason and Drake, she said, "I don't intend for this comment to be rude, but I'm very impressed and surprised that you boys are using silverware. Life on your own for a while can really change a person, but you seem to have as many social skills as anyone in this camp."

"Well, thank you," Jason managed to get out between bites. "Thank you so much for taking us into your society. It was quite a journey just to get here."

"And that is why you're here with me. I wanted to meet with you because you had to face so much adversity to survive. You also have seen much more of the remaining cities then we have."

Drake stepped in, acknowledging, "Well, we had a lot of help. A great man named Fox drove us most of the way. He saved our lives a couple of times, but he was killed in Charlotte. After he'd been bitten by a creeper, he sacrificed himself to take out about thirty more so we could get a head start." He stopped talking and began to look very sad.

Michaela, who was sitting to Drake's right, put her arm on his shoulder reassuringly. She held it there until the younger of the Bennett brothers regained his composure and then finished telling the story of Fox's death. By the end of the story, none of the four people had completely dry eyes.

Marinas said, "It sounds like your friend, Fox, was an amazing person. He helped you get to us, and that would make him a hero in my eyes." By now, everyone was finishing their food, and the waitress reappeared to take the plates away. Conversation was temporarily paused until the table had been cleared. Finally, Marinas spoke again, "So tell me about the supply crates. Our settlement has a pilot who, once a month, makes a supply run to Washington DC, New York City, Atlanta, Philadelphia, and Orlando, just in case there are any survivors. I'm assuming that you were using the supplies. Do you have any recommendations on how the crates could be improved?"

"Well," began Jason, "they were extremely helpful because we could gather food from them as opposed to going into dark, creeper-filled stores by flashlight. I really can't think of anything that would be a good addition because food, weapons, and medical supplies were all we really needed."

Michaela interjected, "I can only speak for the Orlando drop, but I think it would be better if it was consistently in the same place. I'm not complaining by any means, but there was no telling where the crate was going to land from time to time."

Drake nodded. "I agree."

Marinas took a pad of paper and a pen from under the table and began taking notes. "Also, can you share your information concerning the creepers to me? How did you fight them? What do they like and not like?"

Jason and Drake began to recollect anything they could think of about the creepers. Jason pointed out that the creepers in New York seemed to travel in smaller numbers than the creepers in Charlotte. Drake added that creepers were scared of fire and that there were more creepers in areas that had been higher in population before the apocalypse.

Director Marinas sat quietly and took notes on her pad as the boys talked. She occasionally nodded her head, and the whole process went on for several minutes. Finally, after filling an entire sheet of paper from the pad with new information that the brothers had presented about the creepers, she said, "I don't know if you realize how much help you've been already."

Drake replied, "Well, good! I know that we are very grateful to be here, and helping isn't even adequate repayment to express our appreciation."

Marinas nodded. "You all seem very knowledgeable to have been on your own for several years."

Jason grinned at the compliment. "Me and my brother are very well-read. Sometimes, books are the best way to temporarily escape the situation."

"I don't mean to brag," Michaela interjected, "but I'm probably better at Sudoku puzzles than anyone in the world."

Marinas laughed. "If only that meant as much as it used to. I suppose you all three turned out okay." She gave a friendly wink and then leaned forward to whisper, "How well can you three keep a secret?" The director now had a very serious expression, and Jason sensed she meant business.

Michaela replied, "I haven't revealed a secret to anyone in at least three years!" Drake laughed, and she

CREEPERS

continued, "But all joking aside, I think we would be very trustworthy."

"That's what I thought too," said Marinas. "I have a secret to let you in on. Only a few, including your friend, Redman, know about it though, so you have to keep it to yourselves."

"Count on it," Jason responded. "We are a very trustworthy group."

"Good." Marinas spoke just above a whisper, "Although you are among the youngest in the settlement, I feel that you are also among the most knowledgeable regarding the creepers. There haven't been any new additions to our settlement except for you three in over a year, which is why it's so amazing you all arrived together and that our supply drops are working." She stopped for a second, looked around to make sure the room was clear, then continued, "So here's our little secret—there is a medical lab that is connected to this quadrant."

Drake stated, "It's not very secretive. Is that why the armed guard is standing against that wall?" He pointed.

"Well, people know that we have a lab down here," she was still whispering. "The secret is that we have three living creepers inside and that we are working on developing a cure for the virus. They are sedated with drugs, but they are still great test subjects."

The news struck all three teenagers temporarily speechless. They had fought so hard to escape the monsters that plagued their nightmares that knowing there were creepers this close to them, despite being unconscious, was unthinkable. There was no doubt why this had been kept a secret from the rest of the settlement. Finally, Jason got out, "You're working on a cure? Is it close to being discovered?"

Marinas looked hopeful. "We have one of the greatest doctors I've ever met working on it. I think the cure is very close, and I also think that your knowledge will be able to help our doctor, which is why I am telling you this. You know the behavior attributes of creepers better than anyone, and viruses can be cured once the symptoms have been identified. I would like you to meet with Dr. Hashton tonight, and you can discuss this further. This is a great opportunity."

Michaela looked to Jason. "This is so amazing! We can help cure the plague if we work with this doctor! What do you say? Are you game?"

Jason exchanged a look with his brother, and he could tell what he was thinking just by reading his eyes. "We are absolutely in." He looked to Marinas. "If we can somehow help to beat the virus, then we'll do anything. When can we meet with this doctor?"

Marinas took a thick and official-looking notebook from within a desk drawer. She put the notepad she'd been writing on inside of it and then took a planner from within it. She opened the notebook up and appeared to be studying the schedule. "How about you guys get the afternoon off? Go shoot hoops, play tennis, watch movies, or swim. You should relax a bit, and you can meet with Dr. Hashton tonight at six o'clock. I will speak with her about the meeting, and I will tell Sergeant Redman to meet you at your apartment at a quarter to six, okay?"

"That sounds like a great plan," Drake said.

"Good! I am glad you are willing to help us. That is my reason for calling you here, and I am sure that we will be speaking again in the near future."

Sensing the meeting and breakfast was over, Jason stood, and Drake and Michaela followed closely behind. He addressed Marinas one last time, "Well, breakfast was amazing, and I am very excited about meeting with the doctor later."

"I'm glad you enjoyed your food." Marinas now stood too. "Feel free to come back and visit any time that you want to. I will always enjoying talking to you three. Have a good day, and I will probably see you tonight!"

Good-byes were spoken, handshakes exchanged, and soon, the brothers and Michaela were walking down the hallway. They discussed the opportunity at hand and how amazing it would be to help out with finding a cure for the virus.

As they were once again approaching the housing quadrant, Drake asked, "So what do we want to do for the rest of the day?"

Michaela didn't hesitate at all before saying, "I don't know about you boys, but I'm going to swim! Do you know how long it's been since I've been able to relax and get in a pool?"

"Same for us," replied Jason. He looked to his brother. "Remember the last time we went for a swim?"

"Are you talking about when we were being chased down that sewage tunnel by the—"

"That's the time," Jason interrupted before his brother went into any more details.

Michaela laughed and said, "You are so nasty! But I guess I had to do several things that I didn't want to do just to survive." She changed the topic completely and began to tug at her dress. "And I don't know about you, but I feel so uncomfortable in this! I'm ready to find a swimsuit to escape this restriction. I guess I forgot how bad these things were."

An awkward silence fell over the group. Drake said, "Um, yeah. I guess that makes sense." They reached the double doors and went into the housing quadrant, and from there, the merchant quadrant. They all three picked out swimsuits and then another change of clothes before heading back to their apartment. All three had high spirits for the first time in a while.

As they walked into their apartment, Jason said what was on everyone's mind, "I really like being here. It's so nice to feel like I belong somewhere. It's like we have a family here."

"Technically, we are family," Drake mused.

"All right, clever guy. I think you know what I mean."

"Yeah," Drake admitted, "I actually do. And you're right. It's nice to belong somewhere, and I'd almost forgotten what it felt like to go and do something just for fun."

Michaela was heading into the bathroom. "Yeah, let's go swimming! There's no telling what our future holds, so let's have fun while we can. Sorrow can strike at any time."

Jason watched as Michaela disappeared into the bathroom carrying her bathing suit. He didn't want to admit it, but deep down, he knew she was exactly right.

CHAPTER 13

As they headed to the pool, Jason and the rest of his group caused many heads to turn in their direction. He wasn't sure if they were getting more looks because they were new to the area and hardly anyone had met them or because of Michaela. She had gotten rid of the red dress and replaced it with a violet two-piece bathing suit in which she proudly strutted around. Jason glanced at two old men discreetly admiring her from behind magazines they were pretending to read.

It was quite obvious that all three of the teenagers were in incredible physical shape. Not having a seemingly endless supply of food and spending the majority of the day exercising in various ways had made them all extremely fit. They all had next to no body fat at all. The brothers, who were just wearing swim trunks, revealed impressive torsos that looked far too muscular for boys their age. Even Michaela was extremely fit for a teenage girl. Her biceps were obvious, and her abdominal muscles were unbelievably toned. She had very muscular legs for her size; her thighs were almost as round as her waist. All in all, the three teenagers were very impressive physical specimens, and that was probably why so many were looking their way.

Drake was the first of the three into the pool. He dove into the deep crystal clear water and sent a small wake across the surface. There was nobody else in or even near the pool, and as far as Jason could tell, it was hardly ever used, especially at this time of the day. After several seconds, Drake's head popped back to the surface, his dark hair matted to the top of his head. He pushed his hair to the side with one hand while doggy paddling with the other, declaring, "This water feels so good, and it's deep too!" He took another breath and then dove down, disappearing from sight.

Michaela looked to Jason and said, "Your brother is so cute!"

"What do you mean? I swear he's completely insane."

Again, Drake broke the surface, saying, "Hey, I can do a handstand underwater. Watch this!" He breathed deeply and went back down.

"See, he's so funny and adorable!" Michaela pointed at the slightly visible figure of Drake performing a handstand at the bottom of the pool. "I really like him!"

Jason pressed, "Like him as in a romantic interest way?"

Michaela realized how what she said had sounded, and quickly backtracked, "No. No! Not like that at all! I like him in a seems-like-my-little-brother kind of way. He just makes me laugh, that's all!"

Drake gasped as he hit the surface again. "Now that was impressive, wasn't it?" He looked at his brother and

Michaela standing by the edge of the pool and asked, "What the heck are you doing? Get in."

Jason jumped into the pool with no objection. He was surprised by the sharp coldness of the water and the depth of it too. His feet sank down at least eight or ten feet before striking the bottom, from which he pushed up to the surface and said, "Wow! This feels so good!" He'd forgotten what swimming for pleasure felt like. By the time he wiped water from his face and opened his eyes, Michaela was standing on the edge and dipping her foot in the water. He said, "C'mon, Michaela! Get in!"

"It's kind of cold!"

"It feels good once you're in, so come on!" She continued to dip her foot in the pool but didn't appear to be ready to make any sudden moves to get in. In a flash, Jason lashed out and grabbed Michaela by the ankle. She playfully screamed, but he pulled her forward, and she tumbled into the cold water right on top of him. He reached up and caught her in his arms and the two sank under the surface.

When they finally came to the top, Michaela was laughing and holding onto Jason. She said, "You're such a jerk!" That was followed with a splash of water to his face, but she never let go of him.

Things were going great until a familiar voice came from behind Jason, "I hate to interrupt the fun, but Dr. Hashton requested the meeting be moved up for somewhat urgent reasons." It was Redman, who seemed to follow the teenagers everywhere.

Michaela slowly let go of Jason and swam away. She looked at him and Drake, but nobody spoke. Finally, Jason said, "Well, that's no problem. We won't keep the doctor waiting!" He began to swim toward the ladder that hung in the side of the pool where Redman stood. "Do we have time to go change our clothes?"

Redman looked at the swimwear-clad teens and nodded. "I'd imagine that changing is not a problem, but try to hurry when at all possible." Michaela got out of the pool, and Redman looked at her swimsuit before laughing and saying, "I know you probably want to change before you go!"

Michaela smiled. "I've fought creepers in a bikini before! It's not even that bad. That's something you have to do if you're outside every day in the Orlando summer."

Nevertheless, she followed closely behind the brothers as they walked to the tunnel that led back to the housing quadrant. Several onlookers were watching intently by now as Redman called out, "Try to meet me in the political quadrant in ten minutes, and we can go from there." A few people began whispering; it wasn't common that three teenagers were wanted in the political quadrant in a hurry, and that brought speculations about the newcomers.

The group hurried to their apartment. None of them had remembered to bring a pool towel, so they dripped the entire way. Drake was the first to grab his dry set of clothes and hustle to the bathroom. Through the shut bathroom door came a stream of whistling as he began to change clothes. Jason didn't want to sit on his bed in a wet swimsuit, so he leaned against a wall and awkwardly waited for his brother to finish.

Across the room, Michaela had gathered her clothes and appeared to be in the same situation as Jason. She looked up at him and asked, "What are you doing? We've got to change." She turned away from him and reached for the top piece of her swimsuit, calling out, "No peeking!"

Jason quickly dropped his gaze to the floor in front of him and was relieved to hear the door of the bathroom click open. He turned and hurried inside with his clothes and changed. He hung the swimsuit over the shower curtain and put on a snug-fitting maroon T-shirt, tan shorts, and a black belt before hurrying back into the room and putting on shoes and socks. He was relieved to see that Michaela was no longer changing and instead wearing a similar outfit—a light green V-neck and black athletic shorts. Drake wore a loose blue shirt over a white undershirt and looked the most formal of the three.

Jason asked, "Are we all ready to go?"

"Yeah." All three grabbed their assault rifles, knowing that they were soon to come face to face with more creepers, and weapons seemed necessary even if the beasts were sedated. After that they departed, taking a tunnel from the housing quadrant to the political quadrant.

Redman, who stood near the entrance by himself, said upon their arrival, "You were very fast! Nice work. Apparently, this is a somewhat urgent meeting, so I guess we better go."

The teenagers followed Redman through the political quadrant. The tops of a few people's heads were visible in the cubicles. Drake whispered, "Who are these people?" The only head he recognized was the director, who seemed to be focusing intently at paperwork on her desk.

Redman glanced at the five or six heads that were in the room before answering, "Mostly people who help organize supply runs and administer the merchant quadrant or activists looking to present ideas of change or improvement to the settlement." They walked across the room to the door built into the far wall. Once again, the door was guarded by another buff man armed with a shiny rifle and steely expression. Redman nodded toward the man and said, "I'm here to meet with Dr. Hashton."

"Yes, of course." The guard barely looked Redman's direction. He seemed unusually tense. "Go on in."

Redman unlocked the door with a set of keys he had in his pocket and headed inside, gesturing for Jason's group to follow. They did, stepping into the cold room and looking around. Upon first glancing around the room, Jason noted the row of expensive-looking equipment against the wall to his left. There were several medical instruments, although he didn't know what any of them did. The room was dimly lit and, for the most part, empty. A cold chill hung in the air, but no creepers were in sight.

"We have to go through there," said Redman, who pointed toward another door on the far side of the

156

room. He walked to the door and knocked on it, the group standing behind him.

"Come in. It's unlocked." The response came from the other side of the door. The voice was female, but that was about the only notable distinction.

Redman opened the door slowly and walked into the room. The teenagers cautiously followed after him. What they saw inside was breathtaking. Three creepers were lying on small hospital gurneys with their eyes closed. Their only movement was the slow rise and fall of their chest as each breathed. Each of the creepers was hooked to several testing machines, and each had an intravenous medical drip bag feeding some kind of medicine into a port in its arm. Near the three unconscious creepers stood a woman with frizzy red hair, a lab coat, and a bewildered look. She constantly kept looking at the drip bags that were administering drugs to the creepers. Once she saw Redman and his guests, she looked up with a forced smile. "I'm very thankful to see you, Sergeant Redman! And you must be Jason, Drake, and Michaela. I'm Dr. Hashton, and it is an absolute honor to be in the presence of people who survived on your own for as long as you have." She spoke quickly and barely paused between sentences.

"Thank you," Jason replied for the group.

"No problem," Hashton said. "However, I do have a problem, and that's why I requested your help." She stopped, waiting for a response. None came, so she continued, "As you can see, I have these three creepers that I'm experimenting on. I have gathered an incredible amount of information from them, and they are all at different stages of the virus."

That was awarded with the first question. Drake asked, "What do you mean by different stages?"

Hashton replied, "They have had the virus for different amounts of time." She pointed at the creeper on the gurney farthest from the group. "That one has had the virus for four months now. At this stage, the virus has easily had time to finish running its course on the brain, and the host's mental activity is next-to-nothing." She pointed to the next in line. "This one here has had the virus for about eight months now. At about eight months, the change is pretty much complete. The following twelve months seem to be the peak of a creeper's hunting ability, in terms of mental and physical capabilities." She then pointed at the last of the creepers, a smaller and paler one, and said, "This one has had the virus for about two and a half years now. After the peak is over, the virus then begins to work on the nervous system and eventually, it will kill the host. I really don't think this host will live for another two weeks."

"That's very amazing! Does that mean that anyone who contracts the Space Virus will die within about two and a half years?" To Jason, this seemed to be good news. He had always assumed the creepers would live for many years, so he was very excited with the concept of them dying off soon.

"Yes, exactly! That explains why there aren't half as many creepers as there were at first. Most of them have died off, and they all don't have to be killed because they'll eventually die on their own. The only bad news is that the virus has mutated so that it transforms the host much more quickly than it did at first. From what I understand, the first human host took months to change into a creeper. Now, the mutation in the virus has made it so that the host is transformed into a creeper in a matter of minutes." She looked back to the drip bag and continued, "I'm still working desperately to find a cure so some can be saved, but even if no cure is discovered, we should still be safe because we can stay here and wait for the virus to kill off all the remaining hosts. That shouldn't take over a year or two more."

Redman spoke up, "That's the basic idea that this settlement is built around—we can outlast the creepers, and there is even a chance we can develop a cure for the virus to save some of the people that are dying from it. It's hard to remember, but they were once like us too. I try to keep in mind that the Space Virus can change even the best people into monsters."

"Speaking of the cure," Michaela asked, "have you made any headway, doctor?"

Hashton nodded. "I am very close, I think! The only way I could think of curing the virus was to microgenetically engineer a second virus that would essentially kill out the first." She pointed to some equipment in the corner of the room. "I am basically building my own virus that is designed to kill the Space Virus and then die out itself."

Jason said, "Hypothetical situation, you say the virus attacks the brain. If you cure the virus, won't the host still be mentally disabled?"

"That is a great question," Hashton exclaimed, "but the answer is no, thankfully. The Space Virus masks the brains activity as opposed to killing it. The brain is pretty much shut down, but it is still there. I think it will become active once again if I can introduce the new virus into the host." She paused, and then continued, "I hate to be rude, but we don't have much time to discuss this matter now. I need to tell you why I called you here."

"Yes, please do," Redman replied. He sounded as if even he didn't know what the problem was.

Hashton pointed at the creepers. "I figured you've probably noticed that my three test subjects here are in an unconscious state."

"Thank God," Jason said.

"Well, I have them all on a strong sedative to put them in this state." She looked toward the medical drip bag, reached out, and squeezed it gently. The bag was almost empty. "The problem is that I'm almost out of the drug, and if I don't get any more of it, then the creepers will wake up soon. We can't afford for them to wake up because I'd have to kill them. They are such valuable test subjects that it would really set me back in the search for a cure. I know it sounds very irresponsible to run out of the drug, and it probably is, but I've had a lot on my mind."

Redman asked, "So you want us to go find some of this drug?"

"Exactly." Hashton pushed her bangs from her eyes. She then walked over to a table and took an empty box which she handed to Redman. "This is the box that the drug will come in. You'll be able to find it in just about any pharmacy store locally. So what do you say? Will you do it?" She looked each of her visitors in the face with a pleading look in her eyes.

Redman looked to the teenagers. "I know this is a lot to ask on your first day here, but are you in?"

"Of course!" they answered in unison.

"Oh, thank you so much!" The doctor beamed.

Redman asked, "About how much time do we have?"

Hashton studied the drip bag, and then looked back to the creepers, and then Redman. "I'd say maybe up to two hours. I'm going to alert Director Marinas of the situation and get these creepers handcuffed to the gurneys just in case they wake up."

Her answer had brought a sense of urgency. "We better get on the move. I hope to see you very soon, doctor."

Redman turned to leave, but Hashton said, "No, you can go out right here!" She pointed to the ceiling, in which there was a visible hinged door and a tall metal ladder that led up to it. "I had this secret entrance put in so the creepers could be snuck down here. It leads right to the parking lot."

"Great idea," said Jason. He looked at Redman. "We can take our truck." He, Michaela, and Drake all walked toward the ladder that led to the hinged door.

Hashton said, "You really have no idea how grateful I am for your help. I hate having to ask this from you, but know you're doing a great deed. Hopefully, the virus will be cured thanks to you teenagers and Sergeant Redman."

"It's no problem," Jason humbly replied. "We are happy to help."

As they started up the ladder, Hashton pleaded, "Be careful! I wouldn't be able to live with myself if something happened to any of you because of my stupidity. It can be a violent world outside."

Jason led the group of four through the hinged door and out to the Miami night. Nobody spoke, but they were all thinking something similar. With the drugs already wearing off in the sedated creepers, the biggest threat wasn't what was outside of the settlement; the biggest threat came from what was *inside* of it.

CHAPTER 14

"I really want to apologize again for having to ask you to do this," Redman said from behind the steering wheel of Fox's truck. Jason had asked him to drive because he was more experienced with both driving and the area of Miami that they were traveling. Redman continued, "Dr. Hashton has a reputation for being sort of scatterbrained and forgetful, but even this is beyond her typical standards."

Jason, Michaela, and Drake had all squeezed together in the remaining part of the seat, uncomfortably close to each other. They were all clutching their rifles and peering out of the window, looking for any drugstore where they might find the drug they needed.

"Do you have any idea where we can find this?" Michaela held the empty box that Dr. Hashton had given her, and she studied it intently. She tried to read off the name of the drug, but it was too long, so she gave up.

"I know that there is a small drugstore up here a couple miles on the left. That's where we're going."

Redman suddenly stepped on the brakes of the truck and pointed to the center of the street. "Look at that!"

In the middle of the road, there was a long and dark object that Jason had dismissed as a log until it suddenly moved. The long animal opened a pointed mouth to hiss at the truck and reveal incredible rows of teeth. Drake exclaimed, "It's an alligator!"

"Probably came up here from the Everglades," explained Redman. The truck swerved around the enormous reptile, and Redman continued, "After we get the drug, we can send a team back to kill the gator. Fried gator is very popular in the merchant quadrant."

Jason admitted, "I've never seen an alligator before."

Michaela laughed at that. "I killed one when I lived in Orlando. It wasn't as big as that one though."

The truck continued forward and eventually made it to the destination without sighting a single creeper on the journey. Redman pulled into the small parking lot of a little building that read "Antonio's Drugs" on the window. He said, "Before the virus, this place had the absolute best shakes and malts in town. I used to take my son here after school on Fridays, and he'd always get a strawberry shake until—" He abruptly stopped talking and got out of the truck to focus on the task at hand. "We've got to get in there and get those drugs.

Jason and the others got out of the truck as well. He asked, "How are we going to get in?"

Redman, who was carrying a shotgun, raised his weapon, and offered, "Just like this." The gunshot rang out, and one of the glass windows of the store exploded into thousands of tiny shards. The three teenagers all raised their rifles just in case the shot had disturbed creepers hiding inside. There was no movement, so the group continued forward. Redman encouraged, "We have got to move fast if we want to get back to the settlement in time, and I really don't want Dr. Hashton to be forced to kill her test subjects."

"Yeah, especially if she's close to discovering a cure."

The group moved in toward the store with weapons raised. "I'll lead the way," volunteered Redman. "Cover me just in case anything is to happen." With that, he jumped into the drugstore, looked around intently, and then announced, "It's clear. Come on in."

The teenagers all climbed into the building through the window and looked around inside the darkness of the store. It was full of shelves that were covered with packaged foods, medicine, and supplies. Some shelves of medical supplies were only partially full. Just as Redman had advertised, the store had a bar with an ice cream machine behind it. A sign hanging above the bar read, "The best shakes in town." On the far side of the room was a pharmacy counter, and behind that was a shelf on which countless boxes of drugs sat. Redman was already walking in that direction.

"That is a bunch of drugs to look through," said Jason. "How are we ever going to find the right one?"

The group walked behind the pharmacy counter. Redman took something from his pocket and showed it to the teenagers; it was a walkie-talkie radio. He explained, "Several of us have these radios to keep in touch. They are battery-powered and have a five-mile reception radius." He then pressed a button on the radio and said, "Redman for Hashton, Redman for Hashton."

There was a pause, and then Dr. Hashton's voice was audible over the radio, "This is Hashton. How are you progressing?"

"We have found a drugstore, and we're searching for the drug. What kind of time do we have?"

No response came for several seconds. Michaela had picked up a box full of medicine, which she was comparing to the box that Hashton had given them, when the radio came back on. "There can't be much longer. The test subjects are already showing signs that the sedative is wearing off. Their heart rates are increasing."

Michaela exclaimed, "This is it! This is it!" She took the box in her hands and forced it in front of Redman's face.

He excitedly looked between the two boxes and nodded his agreement. Turning the radio back on, he said, "We've got it! We have found the drug you are looking for!"

"That is fantastic news!" That was the reply from Hashton, who then yelled something that was hard to understand through the radio. Once again, her voice became clear, "One of the creepers has awoken. I will try to keep him contained until you can get back here, but hurry!" She sounded desperate and pleading. "Do you copy? Redman?"

Jason had grabbed several more boxes of the sedative drug, and the group started heading toward the truck in a sprint. Redman yelled into the radio, "Hold on! We're coming!" They were moving very fast, running out of the shop and piling into the truck in just seconds. "Where are the car keys?" Redman checked his pockets in a mad flurry.

Michaela offered, "They're in the ignition." She seemed to be the calmest of the group.

"Thanks." Redman started the truck and backed it up quickly. He announced, "Hold on, this is going to be a little wild." He stepped sharply on the gas, and the truck sped forward, turning from the parking lot and onto the street. The truck fishtailed at first, but eventually straightened and continued forward toward the settlement at very high speeds. Redman handed Jason the radio and said, "Hold down the green button and try to make contact with Dr. Hashton."

Jason did as told, pressing the green button and holding the radio to his mouth. "Dr. Hashton? Come in, Dr. Hashton?" Silence.

"Try again."

"This is Jason Bennett for Dr. Hashton. Can you hear me, Dr. Hashton?"

More silence followed. The truck was speeding down the road so fast that the apartment building that housed the entrance to the settlement was already in sight. Still, no response came from the radio. "That is probably not a good sign," Drake said.

"You're right. I really hope nothing bad has happened," Redman added. He continued, "Get your guns ready. We are going in through the front elevator, and we're going to run to the political quadrant to make sure everything is under control." The truck turned so that it was nearing the front entrance of the apartment building.

Suddenly, a response came from the radio, but it wasn't the response that the group was hoping for. The radio was announcing a warning to everyone. Director Marinas was speaking, and a siren was audible in the background. She was yelling, "Code black! Code black! There are two creepers loose in the building! They have escaped the medical compound, and Dr. Hashton has been attacked by them. Evacuate the settlement if possible. If not, gather your weapons because all hell is about to break loose."

The truck screeched to a stop in front of the apartment building. No guard was posted in front of it. The cab had suddenly gone dead silent, and the apartment building now seemed ominous as it loomed over the truck and cast a dark shadow across the street. They all knew that there were two free creepers inside, and two creepers among a large group of unarmed people could quickly go bad.

Redman sighed. "I just can't believe this." He shook his head and got out of the truck. "Everything we did was so safe, and we'd survived for three years here, but now everything has gone wrong. If we go inside, we will probably die, but Director Marinas has done so much for me that I need to save her."

"Don't give up hope," pleaded Jason. "We've been through a lot too, and we can survive anything. Trust us. Think of this as just an obstacle." The teenagers all climbed down from the cab of the truck behind

Redman. Jason walked over to him and put a hand on his shoulder to offer encouragement. "We can do this."

Newfound determination seemed to glisten in Redman's eyes, and he nodded, "You're right, thank you! Now let's go save the settlement!" He ran toward the apartment building suddenly and pushed through the unguarded front doors. Jason, Drake, and Michaela were all at his heels and clutching their weapons tightly, just in case the need for them was to soon arise.

The group ran across the white lobby of the apartment building toward the elevator. Dr. Williams, the man who tested any people entering the settlement for the virus, was nowhere in sight. The lobby was empty and calm, which reminded Jason of the eye of a storm. The biggest question was what was going on under their feet, in the settlement.

Redman pushed the button on the elevator, and the door almost instantly slid open. He stepped in and said, "C'mon, get in."

As the rest boarded the elevator, Michaela asked, "So what is our plan? Where are we going when we get down to the settlement?" The elevator started a slow descent, and the air seemed thick with dread of what was to come.

Redman explained, "The quickest way to get to the director is the key. The elevator takes us to the merchant quadrant, so we'll have to cross that to get to the housing quadrant and, from there, go to the government quadrant. We will have to find Marinas there, and hopefully, we can save her."

Jason spoke as the elevator came to a slow and dramatic stop. "Do you think the creepers have been contained in the medical quadrant? Or could they have escaped?"

"I really have no idea. We never expected anything like this to happen, so we're very unprepared," Redman admitted. "I guess we will see soon enough."

Unfortunately, Redman was correct. As the elevator door slid open, a gruesome sight awaited the self-proclaimed rescue group. The merchant quadrant was completely chaotic. There had to be at least three hundred and fifty people in it, most of which were sprinting toward the elevator. The creepers had apparently arrived because about a quarter of the people in the quadrant appeared to have been bitten and were already transforming into monsters. They had turned into some sort of half-human and half-creeper combination, with skin that seemed to grow paler as the teenagers and Redman watched. The half mutants seemed to already have the hunting instincts of the creepers because they began attacking more of the humans that were attempting to flee.

Jason watched in horror as a fully developed creeper attacked a middle-aged woman who was running toward the elevator. The attacking creeper was carrying a human leg, which he used to club the lady and knock her to the ground before pouncing on her with an open mouth. On the far side of the quadrant, two men were wrestling with another creeper by a rack of clothes underneath one of the merchant tents. The creeper managed to push both men into the rack of clothes before pulling the tent down on top of them. The heavy tent crashed down, and it was obvious that there was no chance the men had survived. The creeper howled in approval. Next, it ran across the quadrant and dove into a younger lady who had to be in her late twenties. Jason looked away as the mouth of sharp fangs flashed down toward the lady, who too was destined to become one of the monsters now. The entire quadrant was full of battles, and the creepers seemed to be infecting humans constantly.

Looking to Redman, Jason asked, "What do we do?" He had to yell the words out to be heard over the commotion.

Redman's eyes were darting around the former market, taking in every tiny detail. The doors of the elevator slid shut with all four still inside. Finally, he spoke, "This elevator is almost our only chance of survival. If we go out there, then we are all but certain to die."

"Story of our life," Drake muttered.

Jason asked, "Are you saying that we should flee?"

"No," Redman answered, "I'm saying that *you* should flee. This is your second day here, and none of this is your fault. Take the elevator up and go find safety. I will go and try to save the director because she's done so much for me." He sounded completely sincere. "Will you do that for me?"

Jason glanced toward Michaela and then his brother. He answered, "No, we can't abandon you. You've been a good friend for us."

"I won't let you follow me. It's suicide. Run and save yourself."

Drake spoke up, "Even if we survive this, what comes next? The rest of the country is a wasteland. There would be nothing left for us. If this is the fall of humanity, count us in too."

The decision seemed final, and Redman forfeited the argument. He looked at each of the teenagers and said, "If you are sure, then let's do this. Stay close!" He pressed a button on the elevator panel, and the door slid open again. By now, even more of the humans were transforming into creepers after being bitten. The half-mutants were attacking humans, creepers, and anything that moved. Redman evaluated the situation, took a deep breath, and then yelled out, "Now's our chance! Run!"

The group sprinted into the chaotic room. They'd only made it about ten yards before a creeper dove at Michaela from her left. It wasn't fully developed. It had the face of a normal woman, apart from its pale skin and yellow eyes. Despite the resemblance to a woman, Michaela didn't hesitate in taking her knife from her belt and slitting the monster's throat to unleash a torrent of hot blood. A small boy was watching. He couldn't have been any older than three, with curly blond hair and a face that was contorted in fear. "Mama!" he cried out the word in terror as he ran to the creeper Michaela had just slain. The boy was a foot from the dead creeper when another of the hideous beasts ran by and scooped him up. He screamed at first but quickly fell silent.

"Keep moving," Jason called out. Drake and Michaela fell in line behind him, and Redman was to their left. They pressed forward through the room, not picking fights but gunning down anything that came too close. There were many dead bodies littering the floor; some were creepers and some were humans that the monsters had been too aggressive with.

Redman stepped over the body of a woman whose throat had been ripped out. He looked sick with recognition but continued forward. Over the roaring of the creepers and the screams of terror from the humans, he yelled, "There are the doors to the housing quadrant! We have to get to them."

The doors were straight ahead, but getting to them was certain to be difficult. In front of Jason, a man came flying through the air and crashing into a wooden table covered with cans of food. The creeper who'd apparently thrown him followed closely in pursuit, diving on the man and biting him on the arm before charging toward Jason with the intent of having another victim. Jason and Drake both sent several bullets in the beast's torso, and it dropped to the ground.

Spying a clear lane to the double doors that could lead to escape, Jason sprinted forward. His brother and Michaela followed closely behind. They passed through the sea of creepers and struggling humans, arriving at the door without being attacked.

As Drake pushed through the doors, he asked, "Do you think the housing quadrant will be infected too, Redman?" No response came, and he whirled around to face the quadrant. "Redman?" He scanned the scene but couldn't locate the sergeant.

By now, Jason and Michaela were looking too. Michaela pointed. "There he is! He's coming!"

173

She was right. Redman was quickly running toward the door. He waved and yelled, "Go on!" A creeper suddenly began chasing him, and he was obviously unaware of the impending danger.

Jason yelled, "Look behind you!"

Redman got the message and turned around just in time to see the monster leap forward and grab onto his ankle. He shook his leg violently, trying to kick the creeper free. He reluctantly raised his gun and put several bullets into the attacker, but by that time, two more creepers were charging at him from behind. As he freed his leg from the dead creeper, Redman was completely oblivious to the two charging from behind. The teenagers watched in horror as the two creepers tackled him. Drake and Jason both shot at the creepers that were on top of their friend, but the effort was too late. Two pairs of sharp fangs dug into Redman's leg, and the sergeant was dragged off into the sea of madness. Bloodstains littered the floor.

All three teenagers stared into the merchant quadrant in amazement. They didn't move at first, until Michaela broke the apparent trance. "We have to keep going. There is nothing we can do for him."

The brothers reluctantly admitted she was right. All hope was gone as they pushed through the double doors and entered into the corridor that would take them to the housing quadrant. The only hope that any of the teenagers had over the past two months had all been vested in Miami, but now the settlement had fallen, and with it, humanity.

As they stared down the empty corridor ahead of them, one word buzzed in each of their heads. Drake was the one who said it. "Alone. Now we're alone." His tone was a blend of mortification and sorrow. "We are absolutely alone in this world."

A positive thought suddenly struck Jason. He suggested, "No, we're not alone." The oldest of the brothers eyed his two partners intently. "We have each other, and that's all it takes." His voice was much more steady than his brother's had been. "Now, c'mon, let's go save the director and get out of here. If anyone can do it, we can."

"You're right," Michaela and Drake agreed. "Let's go!" Together, they turned and ran down the hallway, unaware of the vast horrors that lay ahead.

CHAPTER 15

The group was hurrying down the long corridor with raised weapons. It seemed as though ninety percent of the settlement's population had been in the merchant quadrant, so everywhere else was fairly empty and quiet. Finally, they approached the second set of doors at the end of the hallway. A sign hung above the door. It was black with white letters, and it read, "Housing quadrant."

Michaela leaned to the double doors in an attempt to listen. "Do you think there are any creepers in there? I don't hear any of them."

"There's only one way to find out, I guess." Jason leaned into the door with his shoulder and pushed it open, gun raised. He stepped forward and methodically scanned the room while looking over the barrel of rifle. His entire body was initially tense, but after a few seconds, he relaxed and lowered his gun. "It's clear, or at least it seems clear. C'mon."

Michaela and Drake followed closely behind into the room. Just as Jason had said, it was empty and free of creepers. A quick scan of the long apartments showed that every door was shut tightly, and Jason assumed that there were probably some humans that had locked themselves in their apartments for safety, which was very smart. He finished looking around and then walked forward between two of the long buildings. He kept his gun ready at his side, but the path was temporarily clear.

The sound of a door opening immediately alerted the group. They turned, guns raised, toward the source of the noise, but lowered the weapons once again after realizing the source was an old black man opening the door of his apartment. He was tall and thin, with white hair and wrinkled skin. The man asked, "Are we safe in here?" His voice was hoarse, and he glanced around nervously.

Drake stepped forward, nodding and saying, "For the time being, this quadrant seems safe, but the merchant quadrant is a mess. It's like creeper versus human World War III down there."

The man now stepped out of the room, pulling the door shut behind him. He was still tense, asking, "What on earth happened, son? How did creepers get loose in the settlement?"

"It's kind of a long story," Jason said, "but what matters is trying to keep everyone safe. Do you know how many people are hiding in the quadrant?"

The black man shook his head. "There can't be any more than forty of us. At this time of day, most everybody be at the merchant square or in the recreational quadrant, socializing." He took a second, as if recollecting, then continued, "I was just out here tryin' to get to know the new neighbors, and them creepers come runnin' through the hallway that leads to the government quadrant. There was two full-developed ones and two men that looked like they had just been turned into the monsters. They were actin' like creepers but didn't look the part yet."

"I understand," Jason replied. "It's amazing how quickly the people are transforming after being bitten. The virus is spreading like wildfire in the merchant quadrant because of the large amount of people in it."

"So is everybody down there infected?"

"No, some are dead. The creepers were getting out of hand and killing some, tearing out throats and ripping off limbs. It's not a pretty sight."

The black man lowered his head in sorrow. "I don't know how we're going to get out of here alive. I'm here with my beautiful wife of forty-two years, and I won't let these creepers take her from me. What do you think I should do?" He looked into Jason's eyes. His plea for help was unmistakably sincere. Tears seemed to be welling up in his eyes.

Michaela, who seemed to be the best of the group at calming people down, put her arm around the old man. "It's going to be okay. You can just wait here and hope the creepers kill each other off in the merchant quadrant. As long as you stay in your room, I think you will be safe."

"You're sweet, but we both know that we can't stay in here forever." He looked Michaela in the eyes now, studying the girl. "Where are you all headed?"

Jason answered the question, "We are going to the government quadrant to try to save the director."

He gasped. "You're goin' to the government quadrant? That's suicide! That's where the creepers came from."

"It can't be any worse than the hell we just came through." Jason nodded his head in the direction of the merchant quadrant. "Now listen, there is a secret exit that goes out of the government quadrant. It's a ladder that leads to the surface parking lot that we just used probably an hour ago. If we save the director, we can escape to the upper city. Would you and your wife like to come with us?" He regretted extending the offer knowing very well that the old man wouldn't be able to keep up with the teenagers, but he also knew that it was the right thing to do.

There was no hesitation from the old man. "I'm gonna die one of these days, so if today be the day, then I'm at least going out with a fight." He turned back and opened the apartment door. "Margaret, come here, honey. We're goin' to try to make an escape with these fine children."

An elderly but relatively fit black woman emerged from the apartment, eyeing the AK-47–clutching teenagers. "Are you sure about this, John? Where are we going?"

John answered, "The government quadrant. Apparently, there is a secret exit to the surface there. These kids have offered to help us escape, and I think that this is our best chance."

Jason interrupted, "I'm not trying to be rude, but we have got to go. There are bound to be some creepers that will come this way from the merchant quadrant, so we need all the head start we can get."

"Just a second." John disappeared into the apartment another time. Jason began to worry until the old man came out with two shiny rifles, one of which he handed to his wife. He must have noticed the surprised expression on the boys' faces because he said, "What? Did you not think an old geezer could take care of himself?" He smiled and added, "Lead the way."

The group, now consisting of five, ventured across the quadrant. They walked past the secretary desk where their room had been assigned just two days ago. Jason suddenly became sad after remembering the hope and happiness he'd been feeling earlier that day. Now everything had changed, and all seemed lost. Knowing he had to live in the moment, especially in a time of crisis like this, he forced the emotions back.

They had almost arrived at the double doors that lead to the hallway when John said, "We have company!" He pointed over his shoulder across the room as a streamline of creepers began pouring in from the merchant quadrant. The old man had very keen hearing. He'd noticed the creepers before any of the younger kids.

The creepers were howling, whooping, roaring, and basically making any other frightening sound known to man. Jason whispered, "They haven't spotted us yet. Keep moving," He hunched down and crept forward, but he wasn't quick enough. Thirty pairs of hungry yellow eyes locked onto the group, and they all charged at once. "Screw it! Just run!"

Now the group, including the elderly couple, broke off into a sprint. They ran through the double doors. They were at least one hundred yards ahead of the pack of creepers, but the hallway they entered was easily that long, so the group would be chased down in no time if nothing miraculously changed. Jason looked at the doors behind him as they swung shut. "Does anyone have an extra rifle?" He asked the question with the answer already in his head. The other four people in the group looked to one another expectantly, but nobody offered up his or her rifle. "Well, okay." Jason took his own AK-47 and shoved it through the door handles so as to prevent them from opening. "Maybe this will hold them off." Now without a rifle, Jason took his pistol from his belt and continued down the hallway.

The group was halfway to the government quadrant when the creepers reached the double doors behind them. The beasts attempted to push the doors open, but the rifle that was wedged between the handles kept the doors jammed shut. After the initial push, a second one came. This one was much stronger, and the metal barrel of the rifle bowed but still held the doors shut.

John and Margaret were slowing. Michaela yelled, "Keep going! We're almost there!"

The third pounding to the doors bowed the rifle severely. Both John and his wife had stopped running, instead turning to watch the creepers forcing their way through the doors behind them. They were clutching their sides. Jason pleaded, "We need to go!"

John looked at Margaret and said, "Yes, you do. Go on, my friends."

With one last heave, the doors were blasted open by the incredibly strong beasts. The raging pack of thirty angry creepers charged down the hallway. Still, Jason argued, "No, we won't leave you." The creepers were coming at a full sprint.

"Listen." John had a definitive tone that suggested argument wasn't an option. "You young'ns have a many of years ahead of you. Me and Margaret would slow you down anyway, and the monsters would kill us all that way."

Drake began, "There's no way that—"

"Please go, honey," Margaret interrupted. "Run! Just remember us when you start your own settlement somewhere." She smiled kindly at Jason.

With that, both spouses raised their weapons and unleashed a barrage of gunfire at the creepers. Some of the monsters howled, but Jason wouldn't let his group stay around to watch the show. He wanted to say thank you, but that was nowhere near an adequate expression of how much sacrificing one's life was worth. Not finding the words to say to John and his wife, Jason called out, "Let's go! Run!" He, his brother, and Michaela all made a dash for the doors that led to the government quadrant.

Pushing through the doors, the group stepped into the smallest of the four quadrants. As they looked around the room, all three were surprised by what lay in front of them. The room was completely empty and silent. With the sound of gunfire still chattering in the distance, Jason stepped forward. He called out, "Director Marinas? Are you in here?" He scanned the room more thoroughly. The circle of chairs was empty; the cubicles had been abandoned.

Michaela suddenly pointed to the ground. "There she is Jason!"

He turned to where she pointed and saw the director, or at least her feet that were visible. The rest of her body was concealed behind a cubicle. She was lying motionless. He ran toward her and called out, "Director Marinas! Are you all right?" No response came. He then yelled, "Drake, go and find some medical supplies. She's wounded!" As Jason rounded the row of cubicles, he realized the extent of the director's injuries and mumbled, "Never mind."

What the cubicles had concealed was her torso. As Jason stared down at the director, he realized that Director Marinas's head had literally been torn off by the creepers. A pool of warm blood was spread out on the floor where her head should've been. The sight was gruesome, and he looked away quickly.

Drake asked, "What's wrong?"

"She's dead." Outside, the sound of gunfire ceased, and Jason knew John and his wife had been killed. The situation was looking grim. "We've got to move! Run to the medical lab!" He stood and bolted across the room toward the now wide-open door of the medical lab that had been so tightly guarded before. Drake and Michaela followed closely, nobody saying a word. Behind them, the double doors burst open, and the creepers began filling the room. The savages made terrifying sounds as they spotted the teenagers and began pursuing them intently.

The humans ran into the medical lab, but the creepers were closing in. They turned left and continued forward, past the gurneys and the empty drip bags that had caused this entire problem to begin with. In the dark room, the ladder that ascended to the secret exit loomed ahead. It was their hope in the dark and foreboding situation. Light shone through the exit above into the darkness of the medical room as the sound of creepers closed in.

Jason looked to Michaela and commanded, "You go first. Hurry though." As the girl began to climb the ladder, he turned to peer out the door. The first creepers were already arriving. One's mouth was stained with blood that had come from either John or his wife. That was the first one of the monsters he killed, drawing his pistol and sending three shots right into the blood-covered creeper's stomach. Somewhere in the back of his mind, Jason remembered that fifteen minutes ago, this had been a happy member of the society. He forced the thought out of his head as he watched the creeper's corpse drop to the ground.

Michaela had climbed all the way to the top of the ladder, and she pulled herself through the overhead exit. Drake, who was by now also firing shots into the angry pack, yelled, "Climb, Jason! Go!"

"I'm your older brother," Jason reminded over the constant sounds of gunfire. "It's my job to protect you, so you go, Drake!"

"You have a pistol. I have an AK. I like my odds much better." Drake's point was very clear, and Jason knew that arguing was only wasting valuable time, so he turned and ran to the ladder.

Grabbing a cool metal rung with one hand, he began to ascend the ladder. At the same time that he was climbing, Jason turned and with his free hand began to shoot at creepers that were storming into the room. Several shots were on target and dropped two or three of the monsters. He reached the top of the ladder and yelled, "C'mon, Drake! I'll cover you." Michaela seized him by the hand and pulled him through the secret exit and into the warm Miami evening. Both of them turned and began to shoot through the exit at creepers below.

Drake harnessed his rifle and made a mad dash toward the ladder, grabbing hold, and beginning to climb up as fast as possible. From peering through the hole in the parking lot, Jason estimated that there were about twenty creepers in the medical room with his brother. He continued to shoot as Drake neared the top of the ladder, but there were too many of the monsters below. They were swarming around the ladder, reaching up and slashing the air right beneath Drake's feet. A flow of bullets from Jason and Michaela continued to assault the creepers, but there were just too many. Everything had gone so wrong in a short amount of time. Hope had been replaced with despair.

Drake was near the top of the ladder now. Jason stood above the exit, reaching an outstretched hand toward his brother to pull him from the ladder. Drake saw the hand and then extended his own. He reached out toward his brother and safety, straining every single tendon and ligament in his arm to reach far enough. Still, it was not enough. The brothers' fingertips had barely brushed when one of the creepers leapt up and seized Drake by the ankle with a steely grip. Both brothers stared at each other with wide eyes as the creeper tightened its grip on Drake's ankle. Time seemed to freeze for a brief instant. A reel of memories began to twirl through the back of Jason's mind. He thought about everything he and his brother had faced. They had been best friends, family, and hope for each other just for everything to end this way.

With a tremendous heave, the attacking creeper ripped Drake from the ladder and pulled him down into the pit. Jason tried to yell, but his voice refused to work as he watched his brother fall. He gazed upon the scene in unparalleled horror as his brother was pulled from the ladder and into the room filled with creepers. Drake's arms flailed about as he fell. "Jason!" The cry for help was of no use. He was engulfed by the sea of creepers. They all reached out, arms outspread and mouths opened as he fell within reach. In an instant, Drake was gone. He disappeared underneath the beasts as they jumped on top of their new prize.

"Drake! No, Drake! No…" Jason seemed to have found his voice, but it vanished again in seconds. He was crying enormous tears of grief. Looking down into the settlement, Jason could see the creepers continually flogging his brother. He and his brother had made it through so much that losing Drake hurt even more than death itself. Jason dropped to his knees and vomited onto the asphalt, overcome with relentless grief.

He knew that with every passing second, his younger brother was either being killed or transformed into a creeper—the very thing that he'd spent years killing.

He once again stood up, and this time, he had a purposeful manner in his actions. Jason didn't care about anything anymore. As far as he was concerned, by taking his brother, the creepers had taken him as well. Without any hesitation, he clenched his gun and ran to the edge of the hole, ready to jump. He'd accepted his fate. This was the end.

CHAPTER 16

Jason hung in the air. Looking down, he could see the creepers below. They weren't even paying him attention; all of their focus was going to his brother. Just as he reached the peak of his jump and began to descend, something plowed into him from the right. He was driven sideways and onto the ground, prevented from turning the monster-filled medical lab below into his grave. Jason landed on his back. Michaela was lying on top of him. She'd tackled him to prevent him from jumping, but in the moment of emotion, Jason was mad at her.

"What are you doing?" He yelled through his tears. "Just leave me alone. I want to end this right now." He was sobbing so hard that his chest heaved violently. He tried to push the small girl off of him, but she refused to move.

Michaela was crying too; tears were building up in her pretty eyes, and her face was shiny in the moonlight. Still, she managed to get out, "I won't let you kill yourself now. I loved your brother too, and that's why you can't do this."

With a slightly softer tone, Jason responded, "What do you mean? He's gone! My brother is gone after all of this." He still felt nauseous, and thinking about watching his brother being pulled into the enormous group of creepers only amplified the feeling.

Michaela stuck a bony finger into the middle of Jason's chest. She fought to regain her composure, blinking back tears. Finally, she managed, "Now, listen up and think about your brother. Drake was a hero, and he always kept the will to fight. He was strong in the worst situations, even when there was no light at the end of the tunnel."

"Look at where that got him." Jason had calmed somewhat but was still crying.

Michaela refused to let him win. "Do you really want to end it? Are you determined to go kill yourself? Or can you find the will that Drake would've had to fight?" She knew what she was saying was working, so she pressed, "What would your brother want you to do? Would he rather you be a coward and jump in there with them or would he want you to keep fighting?"

Jason now seemed a little stronger. "You're right. We gotta keep fighting these creepers, if only just to honor Drake."

He started to sit up, but Michaela pushed him back to the asphalt. "I can't let you do that yet. There is one more thing." Jason didn't resist her, but he had no idea what was coming. "I've wanted to do this since the first day I ever saw you," she said. Then Michaela leaned forward and kissed Jason. Their lips met briefly, and he embraced her. After a second, she pulled back and looked embarrassed.

"Thank you," Jason breathed from the ground. He was temporarily in a trance, but he broke out of it and Michaela helped him to his feet. "I've wanted that a lot too," he admitted. "And now let's get out of here. They'll be coming for us soon."

Michaela was already on the move. Nearby, in the parking lot, was a rolling dumpster which she tried desperately to push, yet it wouldn't budge. She looked to Jason. "Come give me a hand."

Jason ran to the dumpster. "Where are you pushing this?"

She answered, "We need to roll it over the exit. It won't stop the creepers, but I promise it will slow them down."

He knew she was right, so he leaned into the dumpster and pushed with as much force as he could muster. The rusted wheels squeaked hesitantly but decided to start rolling, and after the initial push, the dumpster rolled fairly smoothly. They pushed it quickly, and soon, it was in place above the exit, temporarily sealing the creepers underneath. As the rolling dumpster came to a stop, Jason tried hard to not think about what he'd done, but moving it seemed symbolic of saying farewell to his fallen brother.

Tears were beginning to form in his eyes once again, but Michaela interrupted, "We have got to run. You know they'll be after us soon." With perfect timing, the sound of creepers striking the bottom of the dumpster rang out into the still night.

Jason began backing away. He asked, "Where are we going?"

Michaela glanced around the parking lot. "Check and see if any of these cars are unlocked and with keys to start them." It was a brilliant idea, but unfortunately, it didn't work out. They hurried from car to car, but none were unlocked. Another squeaking sound pierced the night. "What is that?"

Jason replied, "The creepers are rolling the dumpster from on top of the exit. We have to go—now!" He grabbed her on the arm and pulled so she'd give up trying to find a vehicle. With no other choice, they began to race across the parking lot and down a Miami street. They had only made it two hundred yards from the exit when a loud and triumphant roar let the two friends know that the creepers had made it out of the lab and into the city. Both Jason and Michaela were very fast, but they were no match for the speed and hunting instincts of the group of creepers.

Nevertheless, they pressed forward, jumping over curbs, dodging benches, and avoiding light poles. Neither of them had the slightest idea of where they were going. They just ran to escape—to live. Exhaustion crept in, clenching a tight clasp around Jason's chest. His ribs hurt, his lungs felt empty, and his vision was blurring. Michaela was in front of him, but she was slowing too. The pursuing creepers never seemed to get tired, their howls and roars were steadily getting closer and closer.

"Turn here," Michaela wheezed. "Maybe they'll lose our trail." Both humans knew that wasn't going to happen because creepers always found their prey. Still, they turned from the street and ran down an alley.

In the alley, Jason spotted a service stairwell that scaled the side of the building to his right. He asked, "Do you want to climb this? Maybe we could trick them."

She shook her head. "If they could climb the ladder to get out of the medical lab, then they could chase us up there too. Let's keep going."

Jason said, "How far have we run?"

"I'm not sure. Probably about two miles. I'm so tired Jason."

Jason was gripping his pistol. He asked, "Should we try to stop and fight them?"

"No, that's suicide. You don't even have a rifle." With that, she took off again, sprinting down the alley and fighting off exhaustion. Jason followed, but he just wanted to lie down on the asphalt underneath his feet. He didn't even care if he were to get up ever again. In the back of his mind, he had already accepted both his and Michaela's inevitable fate. The creepers were progressively gaining ground, and there was no way to escape.

After several painstaking seconds, the end of the alley came into sight. The friends ran out of it and into the light. Jason gasped at what lay in front of him. To his left and his right, as far as he could see, an expanse of beach stretched out to the horizon. There was so much sand, and there was an enormous expanse of ocean on the far side of the sand. The end of the land meant the end of Jason and Michaela, and they both knew it. An unspoken understanding formed between the two friends.

"Well, I've always wanted to swim in the ocean, and I guess now is my chance."

"Let's go for a swim."

Both teenagers were staring death in the face, just as they had for the majority of their lives. This time, death was certain though, and Jason felt that how he faced it determined if he was a hero or a coward. It was something he'd learned from Fox—times of trial define a person. The response to the adversity is what decides who is weak and who is strong. He refused to back down to the fear of death, taking off across the hot sand in a final sprint to the expanse of water in front of him. Jason turned back to Michaela. "I'll race you to the ocean!"

When he turned around, he saw the stream of creepers flowing from the alley where they'd just come from. The hideous beasts seemed to come in endless numbers; there had to be at least two hundred and fifty of them. It appeared that every last creeper from the settlement had joined in on the pursuit.

Jason decided to look ahead rather than focus on what was behind him. He and Michaela ran through the sand, fixated on the beauty of the ocean illuminated by the colorful sunset. They both laughed, somehow delighted by such a fitting ending. Most people their age would've been angry, feeling as if they'd been cheated out of life. The two friends, however, realized that they'd been blessed to survive as long as they did.

Jason knew he was soon to share the same fate as his brother, but he was accepting that.

The water was surprisingly cool. Jason and Michaela ran into it until it lapped at their ankles. She splashed to him and gave him a hug, saying, "I'm sorry things ended this way, but thank you for making the last few days of my life great!"

Jason hugged her back and replied, "The same goes to you, and I know that Drake would've agreed with us completely if he were here."

The words came spoken too soon. As Jason and Michaela turned to welcome the attacking creepers, the creeper leading the pack was unmistakable. It had Drake's face, his build, his clothes, and even his smile. The difference was that this time, the smile revealed jagged fangs, and his eyes glistened a sinister yellow.

Jason yelled out, "Drake, don't do this!" The mutant face of his brother showed no emotion. Drake didn't slow, only gained speed if anything. The creepers had formed something of a wall that was steadily moving closer to the two remaining humans. They bounded nearer with every passing second, and in the heat of the moment, Jason made a realization that had never occurred to him before. He looked around at the charging monsters, and to his amazement, he recognized several of them. One to his right was the old man who had given them bread in the merchant quadrant—what had his name been? Another one of the creepers was obviously the housing quadrant secretary, Ms. Johnson. She still had her spectacles on, but they were slouching on her nose to the extent that they did no good for her piercing yellow eyes.

"Look," said Michaela as she pointed at another creeper. "That's Redman." She was right, of course. The creeper was unmistakably the mutated version of the man who'd helped them with so much. He walked with a limp, but the source of the faulted gait became apparent when Jason saw that a large chunk of flesh had been bitten out of his leg. Bone was visible, and the wound was bleeding, but somehow, Redman didn't care. He ran his tongue across rows of fangs as he advanced.

The monsters were ninety feet away when Michaela finally asked, "Are we going to fight them?"

Jason's eyes locked onto the creeper that had been his brother only minutes before. Drake continued to press forward with a hungry look in his eyes. "No," he finally answered. He looked at all of them and realized that they weren't his enemies; they were his future. Everything that he'd ever thought during the past three years seemed to be fallacy. He and his brother had put so much time and effort into killing the mutant humans, but now, that seemed wrong and even almost inhumane. He told Michaela, "These aren't the monsters we think they are. They can't help it. They're just sick people. They were just unlucky and caught the virus, but it's not their fault." She nodded understandingly. At this time, they'd been enlightened; everything seemed to make sense.

Both Jason and Michaela dropped their weapons. Jason took his friend by the hand, interlacing fingers with her, and staring at the creepers as they stormed forward. She looked at him. "Thanks again."

He smiled. "Yeah, you too." Jason then looked back at the creepers and yelled as loud as he could, "It's all right! It's okay! I realize that you can't help what you're doing and that you're just unlucky to be sick." He turned to his mutant brother, who was feet away with an open mouth ready to spread the virus. "You're the best brother I could have asked for, Drake. You mean the world to me, and I love you a lot. I want you to know that." Now he spoke collectively to the pack, "Now come and get us!"

The creepers stopped. Completely unexpectedly and abruptly, they all froze in place, digging their heels into the sand of the beach and ceasing their attack. Jason was even more amazed when the enormous wall of creepers took three or four steps in retreat.

"What the heck?" Jason was completely awestruck. "Do they understand me? Are they scared of me?"

Michaela violently shook her head, looking back and forth between the creepers and Jason. "I'm not trying to be rude, but they aren't listening to you at all."

He studied the creepers and was surprised to see that all of the pairs of yellow eyes were looking past him and into the sky. The faces of the creepers were now displaying an expression Jason had never seen on a creeper before—the creepers were showing fear. Their eyes were wide, and their mouths were clenched shut. "What are they scared of?" Jason had no sooner rolled the sentence from his tongue when he heard the roar coming from behind him. The sand on the beach suddenly began to blow into the air, getting in both of their eyes and noses. Fortunately, the creepers were surprised by the sudden gust of wind too, and they all reeled back, covering their eyes.

Jason had no idea what was going on, and things even got more confusing when the sound of gunfire erupted from behind him. Powerful shots rapidly slammed into the earth and ocean, throwing even more sand into the air. He dove, grabbed Michaela, and threw himself on top of her to shield her from the blasts. All the creepers roared at the same time, unleashing an enormous blast into the evening. They looked contemptuously at the object that had terrified them before the entire pack of over two hundred retreated back toward the city and away from the beach. Jason watched his mutant brother fleeing toward the city and wondered if he'd ever see him again. There were so many unanswered questions.

As he and Michaela lay on the beach, water lapping up around them, they watched the creepers retreat. Michaela asked, "What on earth scared them off?" She had to yell to be heard over the continuous roar coming from behind them, but the roar was dying down slightly.

Jason shook his head, afraid to look behind him. "I'm not sure." The wind had now subsided, the gunfire ended, the sand had calmed, and the roar had been extinguished. "What could be scary enough to make two hundred creepers run away?"

The next thing came completely unexpected. The voice of a third human called out from behind where Jason lay on Michaela. The voice was male and seemed to chuckle with good humor. "I don't think I'm *that* scary, and it looks like I got here at the perfect time." The voice caught the friends off guard, but they both turned at once, and suddenly, everything made sense. A large black helicopter, mounted with a gun turret on the side, had touched down on the beach. Its propellers were still spinning but already slowing. A man in military clothes and holding a rifle had jumped down to the sand and was walking toward Jason and Michaela. He said, "I'm James Holder and I'm on a rescue mission from Australia."

Of all the possible things that Jason could say, something completely unexpected poured out of his mouth, "I know you!" He blurted out the statement before he had even placed the man, and then figuring out just where he had seen the man, he continued, "You are Fox's brother-in-law!"

"You know Fox? Is he alive?" The military man now seemed even more interested in the teenagers.

"He was until three days ago. He sacrificed himself to help my brother and I get to the Miami settlement, but then it was overtaken with creepers, and they even took my brother before chasing us to the beach." Jason was still very sad, but his mind seemed to be more in shock than in mourning as he pointed at the retreating creepers.

"Well, I think I have some good news," Holder said. "Don't give up yet. Australia has beaten the virus. We have a population of five thousand, and most importantly is that we have a cure."

The simple sentence changed everything, and an enormous well of hope began filling Jason and Michaela.

They had so many questions, yet none seemed to come out right.

Fortunately, Holder did the talking, "Ever been to Australia?"

"No," they answered together.

"Well, I think it's about time. I have so many things to ask you two, but I think it will have to wait. For now, come with me." Jason stood from the water and then helped Michaela to her feet. Together, the three boarded the helicopter, where the two wet teenagers were given towels before being introduced to the pilot. The helicopter's powerful engine was started, and Holder continued explaining, "Australia has set up a temporary colony in Georgia, looking for survivors in the United States. So far, you are all we have, but you might be just what we need. It's hard to hear over this beast, but I will explain much more in just a bit. For now let's get to safety."

After he and Michaela sat down in the very back, Jason stared out the window of the helicopter as it rose. He saw his now fully-mutated brother vanish back into the alley that the creepers had come from, and at that point, he swore to himself that he would get Drake back no matter what the cost.

"I can't believe this." Michaela broke his train of thought. "What do you think will happen to us?"

"I'm really not sure," Jason admitted, "so I guess we'll just have to trust this man and see where he takes us." They were sitting in a second row of seats in the back of the helicopter, behind their newest ally. Jason put his arm around Michaela, and she leaned into him. They looked out the window, finding happiness among all of the misery that had befallen them. He was still feeling physically sick over losing Drake to the creepers, but now there was a newfound hope that he could get his brother back. Finally, Jason summarized the moment, "I thought that it was over for us, and that fighting creepers was the whole point of our life. I thought our adventure had come to an end, but now, I can see it's just beginning."

They leaned back into the seat as the helicopter flew into the darkening sky, unsure of where their journey would take them next, but certain that they would be ready.

END OF BOOK ONE

ACKNOWLEDGEMENTS

Wow, what a ride. That's the best way to put it. This whole roller-coaster ride of the publishing process—from conceiving the idea to finally marketing my book—has been absolutely crazy, stressful, hectic, and busy. That being said, the process has been worth every second of it. I probably just put way too much stress on myself, but I know that is the best way to deliver a successful story. I take pride in my work and always try to do everything to the best of my ability. That being said, nothing I have done would have been possible on my own. I owe thanks to so many people, and here are just a few.

First and most importantly, I want to thank God for everything He has done for me. I know that all of my talents are gifts from Him and that I shouldn't waste any of them. He has always been there for me, and he constantly bestows blessings on me even though I have let Him down countless times.

Next, I would like to thank my family. My parents have been extraordinarily supportive of my crazy little dream of writing a book and I hope that I never let them down. I love you both and appreciate everything you do for me. I probably don't say that enough.

I would also like to thank my teachers—past and present—and the influence they have had on my life. A good teacher should never be taken for granted, and they play such an important role in one's education. Most of my teachers have been so encouraging of my dream and they are a gigantic part of this book. I couldn't have made it here without any single one of them, but I only can name a few. Mrs. Reed, my kindergarten teacher, who saw a creative mind in a little boy's hand-drawn picture "books." Mrs. Branscum showed me how to love writing. In fourth grade, after she called me her "future author," I told myself I'd dedicate my first book to her. All of my higher level English teachers were important too—Ms. Tharp, Ms. Morgan, and Ms. Bardin. They taught me the skills to write my ideas down and convey them in a way that they made sense.

The Tate staff has been a huge blessing to me too. They were all so helpful and supportive, and they made the entire process a pleasant one. I really enjoyed working with my team. It was great working with Ms. Canillo, my project manager. I also had a great editing crew. I would hate having the job of cleaning up after me, so thanks for doing it so well! It was also an honor to meet Mr. Tate. He is a great man and it's an honor to have the family name on my book.

Additionally, I would like to thank my friends for the support I have had along the way. Grant Eastman, my best friend, has been a huge proponent of my writing and I appreciate that immensely. I owe thanks to

Trace Cooper, too, who could make me laugh even on the most stressful of days in the process. And lastly I'd like to thank Tristan Loveless, who offered constant support and ideas. He is a brilliant mind and is undoubtedly going to be extremely successful someday, so remember me when you're a multi-billionaire.

Thanks to my characters, who did pretty much anything I asked of them without complaining.

Lastly, thank you to all of my fans. Please share this book with someone else (preferably not physically). I write my best for all of you and I hope this novel is the first of many. Maybe one day I can be on the New York Times Bestseller list. That is my ultimate goal. None of it would be possible without your support.

May my stories bring you an escape to adventure,
Jesse Haynes